Autant

Autant

PAULETTE DUBÉ

Paulette Dubé

Chère Claire —
Vous êtes un ange — Be best kind
😊 ,

J t'aime x P

thistledown press

Thistledown Press Ltd.
410 2nd Avenue North
Saskatoon, Saskatchewan, S7K 2C3
www.thistledownpress.com

Library and Archives Canada Cataloguing in Publication
Dubé, Paulette, 1963–, author
Autant / Paulette Dubé.
Issued in print and electronic formats.
ISBN 978-1-77187-156-3 (softcover).— ISBN 978-1-77187-173-0
(HTML).— ISBN 978-1-77187-174-7 (PDF)
I. Title.

PS8557.U2323A94 2018   C813'.54   C2018-901135-1
C2018-901136-X

Cover and book design by Jackie Forrie
Author photo by Raymond Blanchette-Dubé
Printed and bound in Canada

Canada Council   Conseil des Arts
for the Arts   du Canada

Thistledown Press gratefully acknowledges the financial assistance of the Canada
Council for the Arts, the Saskatchewan Arts Board, and the Government of
Canada for its publishing program.

Autant

Confiteor

I confess to almighty God, and to you, my brothers and sisters, that I have sinned through my own fault, in my thoughts and in my words, in what I have done and what I have failed to do; and I ask blessed Mary, ever virgin, all the angels and saints, and you, my brothers and sisters, to pray for me to the Lord our God.

Families from Autant

Garance: Edgar and Lucille (née Corneille)
children: Alice, Juliette, Maurice and Bella

Corneille: Joseph (brother of Lucille) and Léah

Trefflé: Philip and Émérentienne
children: Fernande, Germaine, Marcel, Suzanne, Alexandre, Eustache, Adrien

Toupin: Hector and Florence
children: Séraphin, Estelle

(2012)

Garance: André (youngest sibling of Alice, Juliette, Maurice, Bella)
children: Léo, Pierre, Urbain

Robichaud: Alice (née Garance): married Adrien Trefflé — deceased, and Roland Robichaud — presumed deceased

If heaven is full of angels like me, hell must be empty.
— letters from Autant

GOD AND RUEL ARE SITTING at a dark table in a bar. It is late, later than either realises. They are nursing warm beers and heavy into their conversation, heads nearly touching, shoulders hunched. The bartender brings up a couple of tequila shots. "This is from the lady in the corner." He winks.

Ruel and God look over and lift their glasses in her direction. She raises her martini glass and together they drink to one another's prosperity. Ruel turns back to the table with a sigh and picks up his tankard.

God says, "If I wanted you dead, you would be."

"You should you know. Extinguish this miserable flame."

"Why?"

"To punish me."

"I don't do that."

"You must. I have shame, such guilt."

"Shame or guilt?"

"Either, both. I was distracted and rather than gently pushing the soul, I pulled it too quickly and it exploded like slapping mercury."

It's a push, not a pull. Will they never get that right? God sighs, shakes his head and says, "You did as I asked, no more, no less."

"I followed your command, I did not fulfill it. For that . . . "

"For that, you wish to erase yourself?"

"I am untrustworthy."

"You know nothing. Guilt, shame, punishment . . . you have lost the essence of everything if you are using these words."

"I am lost."

"Ruel, look at me. Look. At. Me."

Ruel lifts his head and looks into God's eyes.

"There is only love. You are made of and for love. That is what this is. There is nothing else."

Ruel opens his mouth but God raises a hand to stop him. "Find a way. Go back and find a way. Oh, and Ruel?"

"Yes, Lord?"

"Don't be distracted. No fucking cheating."

"Yes, Lord."

From a stool at the bar, Coyote watches the angel walk out. He lights a cigarette, picks up his beer and crosses the floor. The lady with the martini glass looks up. He sits across from her, touches her hand. "It's time." He blows smoke.

"Yes," she says.

Coyote cocks his head. "You need to remember one thing while you are down there."

"Oh? Just one?" She smiles a little crookedly. Taking the cigarette from him, she draws on it and blows a perfect square.

He laughs. "Remember, the light is different. Your perception will be blurry at the best of times. I call it being lightheaded. Anyways, trust the bees, they know how to navigate. If all else fails, follow the bees."

"Bees," she repeats, putting the cigarette in the ashtray. She stands and pulls on her cloak. "Got it."

Coyote sighs.

He goes up to God's table. God sees him coming and juts his chin towards the empty chair. Coyote sits down.

Bee Log
Edgar Joseph Garance
1946

Am writing down everything, so the next one will do this right.

janvier — morning snow, cloudy and mild
Have hives (2) made. Need 10 frames: 3/8" space on all sides, any smaller and the bees will fill it in. Bees will arrive from Illinois, America. Hope they like it here.

Queen's stinger can be used many times. If you are ever attacked by many bees, drop your gaze and seek cover. There is something about our eyes they don't like. One mad bee will call another 30 guards to chase you away. Be gentil and you will be quite safe.

février — clear, cold
Rigged the tub for warming and spinning the frames. Wheel on the floor.

mars — clear, cold, clouds over and snows
Lucille's a little anxious about the bees. I told her bees here in the North Americas came from a French man, Camille Pierre Dadant, he moved to Illinois in 1863. That made her happy. To know that bees are French was a relief, because she will be able to talk to them!

13

In any case, they won't bother her; they have their hive to attend to. The queen bee is quite shy after all, much bigger than the worker bees and always has attendants to feed and care for her. The males or drones have only one job to do, and mate only once in the lifetime of the queen. If the queen decides to lay an egg for another queen to split the colony, she makes certain there are males available for mating; otherwise she destroys all the attendants, *vièrges* they call them — by singing a certain song. If they answer her, if they sing back, she barges into the cell and kills them off.

avril — snow, cold wind

Pollen from the pussy willows, elm and other trees will be good for hatching bees. Lucille set up a little altar to Saint Bernard de Clairvaux — patron saint of beekeepers and candle making. I told her I wasn't too sure if the bees will be Catholic. She said, If they are French, they are Catholic. It's good to know that Bernard de Clairvaux will intercede on our behalf to Marie. The bees should arrive in mai, the month of Marie.

mai — cold, cloudy, windy, some rain

Queen arrived with 3 lbs. of bees. Every second one is dead, including the second "just in case" queen. The first queen looks good.

Placed the hive: bees need water and food, away from people. They will forage 3-5 miles from the hive. Entrance facing South-South-East.

Hung frames, hope for the best. They will work to make their own wax. Supplement with sugar sirop. When there is an excess of honey or sirop, the bees will digest the honey and produce wax.

Recipe for mead: came with the bees

Have at the ready: 4-gallon fermenter, 15 pounds of honey, 5 gallons of clean water.

Here are some things that are nice to have: seasonal fruit, glass carboy with airlock.

Put 2 gallons of water into your fermenter. Mix in all of the honey vigorously with a slotted spoon or a whisk.

Pour in the remaining water and stir vigorously for a few minutes to aerate the solution. Now you have a "must". This is the solution of honey and water before fermentation has occurred.

For a fruity mead, add 5 pounds of fruit and stir vigorously, making sure the chopped pieces of fruit are completely covered in the must.

Once the fruit has been mixed in, firmly secure the lid of your fermenter and add the airlock.

Place the fermenter in a cool dark place. Twice a day, you should remove the lid and vigorously stir the must. After about five days of stirring, your must should be fermenting. You will be able to tell by the foamy head of carbon dioxide bubbles on the top of your must and the bubbling in your airlock.

When your must reaches this stage, remove any fruit you have floating around in your fermenter.

After another week of fermentation in your sealed fermenter, you will have fresh sweet mead. Pour this right into your cup. It will be fruity, sweet, and effervescent. You can also bottle it and refrigerate for consumption over the next couple of weeks.

If you are planning to let your mead sit for more than a couple of weeks, then it would be better to use a secondary fermenter. As with brewing beer, the best secondary fermenters are glass carboys. Once you plug your carboy with a bung and airlock, the mead is free to ferment and mature. You can leave it there for months.

Once in the bottles, store them in a cool dark place and drink at your leisure.

juin — cloudy, strong wind

Avoid opening the hive on cold, windy days, because all the field-working bees are at home and unhappy not to be working.

juillet — low pressure moving in, sinus pain, joint in the arch of my foot

Bees, unless you squeeze them, will seldom sting you. I don't wear gloves, too clumsy, but it is still wise to wear a veil to protect your eyes — eyes they don't trust. If they should get annoyed with you because you are too rough on them, before they attack you will notice *la senteur humaine*, warning you. A few puffs of smoke from a smoker or a pipe will usually settle them (and the beekeeper) down.

août — clear, warm, windy and dry

If conditions are right, food supplies and all, the queen can lay a thousand eggs in one day. Get a chicken like that and I could be rich!

15 lbs. of honey this month! Couple of jars to the neighbours and combs for the kids for a treat.

I have a new daughter, Bella Marie. Born Monday, August 26. Madame Trefflé and Léah are helping out.

septembre — light snow in last part of month, then dry, cold

Actual main honey flow was only for a couple of weeks. This colony can bring in 50 lbs. of nectar a day. Kids and dogs like it, makes it easier to clean up the shack.

Saw a bunch of drones outside the hive, wandering aimlessly. They are evicted it would seem . . . wonder what they did to piss off Her Majesty?

Have to keep the bees fed in winter, they have some food stored in there, but made up a batch of sirop for them to drink. Recipe for the sirop: 2 lbs. of sugar, 1-pint water and brewer's yeast for protein.

octobre — cloudy, warm, clearing and colder

Kept some honey in the hive for winter bee food.

novembre — very cold, hazy mornings, dry near end of month

Hand tarps over hives. Supplement with sugar sirop.

Lucille's happy with the candles that she and the girls made. They smell pretty, different from tallow candles. She gave some to the priest for the church and left us a few for our St. Clairvaux statue and Sainte Marie.

AUTANT, 2012

ALICE'S SECOND HUSBAND DIED ALMOST five years ago. She relies on her brothers, Maurice and André, to fix the things that need fixing over at her place. It is only a matter of course that they should be called to look at the roof, but she doesn't want to bother them right away. She waits until the rainstorm has wept itself dry, sweeping through Autant, moving away, down south towards Edmonton.

Maurice comes first, tiptoeing up and over buckets, pails and roasting pans strategically placed from one end of the house to the other. He looks up at spider cracks running the length of the house. He taps his nail against the doorframe in time to the syncopated plinks and plops of rain dripping into the galvanized bucket just inside Alice's bedroom.

"Alice," he says, "the roof is leaking."

"Maybe because of the storm," Alice says.

"Probably," Maurice says. "Storms tend to be full of water."

"Yes, especially when it rains hard and long," Alice says. "Or in the spring when the snow melts, there's water. Did you check the eavestroughs?"

"Yes, yes I did. They're choked with leaves and junk. I could see them kind of sagging from the driveway when I drove up. You get those cleaned out since we did them a few years back?"

"Roland was going to get to it, but . . . "

"I know, I know, he died." Maurice touches his sister's hand. "We'll get up there first thing. Don't worry. I'll call André and the lumber company and . . . "

"But that will cost money! I mean, you could just clean out the eavestroughs and re-patch the ceiling couldn't you? You two are so good at that sort of work. There is no need to buy lumber and all."

Maurice listens to the rain plink plonking down the hall. He cocks his head and watches the plaster heave and give a little more above the toilet.

"No patching this time. No, not this time, Alice. This time, we rip it off and begin again."

André, their youngest brother, climbs the ladder two days later, garden hose tucked into the extra loop of his tool belt. He expects leaves and bird shit gone to sludge. He expects the odd bone, nest or dead bird. As he sprays and scoops, prods and swears at the mess, he is stopped by a whiff of rotting fish gut.

"What in the Sam Hill?" he says, his eyes watering at the nasal assault.

He leans an elbow on the eavestrough and gags. In reflex, his hand shoots out and grips the eavestrough. It gives way, opening like a zipper, pulling away with sickening ease from the rotted two-by-fours. Panicking, André brings his other hand up to support the pitted tin. He only succeeds in knocking more of it loose.

"Maurice! Chrissake do something! The whole thing . . . "

Before he can finish, before Maurice can even start laughing properly, André falls from the ladder and the whole northeast side of the eavestrough comes squealing down. One solid piece, welded together by the intrepid Roland, connects with Maurice's forehead and sends him sprawling into the caragana shrub.

Alice sets the platter of sandwiches down with a thump. "I don't know what happened. That should have never fallen away like that. Rolly welded . . . "

"Alice, I know. It's all right." Maurice bites into his first fried egg sandwich.

André eases his way onto a chair.

"How is your bum?" Alice asks, pouring tea into his cup.

"Oh jim-dandy." He lifts one cheek then the other, trying to find the spot that hurts the least.

"That damned ladder," says Alice. "That ladder was rickety the day we bought it. I told Roland that. I said, 'Roland, that ladder feels rickety to me. Unstable. I am afraid someone will fall.' And look! Someone fell and got bonked on the head."

She turns away from the table and glares at the old wooden ladder through the kitchen window. Maurice rolls his eyes and picks up another sandwich. André sighs, putting down his mug of tea.

"You know," he says, reaching for a sandwich, "there is something in the roof."

"Yes," says Maurice, "bats."

"Nope, not bats, something else. Something smells bad in there."

"What? Oh, musty, einh? Mould maybe?"

"No, hell no. Way worse than that, I tell you. Smells dead and rotting."

André pulls apart the sandwich and sniffs each side of bread, a childhood wont. Alice returns to the table laden with fruit cocktail and Dream Whip, her grudge against the ladder forgotten.

"Anyone for dessert before you get back to work? Oh, did I tell you? Doris called from town. Remember those moths we had a few days back? Before the storm? Well, apparently, she said that the hospital shovelled 1000 pounds of those moths from the entrance. And she said the school bagged 1,500 pounds because Madame Nault left the light on in the foyer after she left. Moths trying to get to the light. That's nearly 3000 pounds of moth! I wonder where they came from? I know where they got to. Thank God the rain washed most of them away. 'That is amazing!' I told Doris. 'That is . . . '"

"That is what's in the roof," André says.

They decide to go at it from the inside since they don't know how stable the roof is. First, they haul Alice's furniture out of the living room onto the front lawn.

"Having all my things out there in plain view of the whole world!" she says. "It's not decent."

"Who is going to see it way out here, Alice? You expecting a parade maybe down the driveway?" asks Maurice.

"You can cover it up. You have blankets and sheets and stuff don't you?" asks André.

"Of course I have sheets, but I am not going to put them out for the world to see!" she says. "That's why clotheslines are in the back of the house, Monsieur André. Not everyone needs to see . . . "

" . . . that she hasn't bought new sheets since before old Rolly died," says Maurice under his breath.

Alice has already started back towards the house, calling back about getting old clothes to protect their good clothes while they work.

He wipes the sweat from under his nose and signals André to stop and have a smoke. "This is going to go down as the summer that never was," he said, as he stiffly lowered himself into the dusty red velvet wing chair.

"What do you mean?" André plucks a long stem of grass gone to seed and sticks it in his mouth.

"Are we ever going to get out of this mess long enough to go up to Winagami Lake, do you suppose?"

"Ah, the fish'll wait. Alice's roof? Well, I wouldn't bet the farm on it being here after one more good rain. We've let things slide, Maurice."

"We, let things slide? What do you mean slide? Who was out here every year to change the storm windows? Who painted the kitchen after that little accident with the deep fryer? Who put in the new toilet and the new linoleum in the living room and got the phone hooked up?"

"All right, all right, Maurice, calm your nerves, old man. Have your smoke. Jésus you are touchy today."

"Well, a conk on the head has pushed aside my jollies, I guess. And I don't like the idea of spending my summer cooped up with Alice and her ghosts and her Roland and Christ-knows what all else is up in that attic. I am not looking forward to those moths. How are we supposed to get rid of them once we get them out anyways?"

"Fire," says André.

"Come again?"

"We burn them. I already asked the boys to come over later on this afternoon to help clean up the mess I figure we'll have with the roofing. They will bring wheelbarrows and another garbage barrel if she doesn't want to use the garden. We burn the whole stinking shebang."

"The kids will do that for you?"

"Yep. For the love of their old man," says André.

"How much?"

"Twenty bucks each for the job, plus I take them to supper on the weekend at the Café."

"Good enough. Let them do that work then."

"A shit-load of butterflies up there that's all," says André.

"Well, I don't want to be underneath a shit-load of dead anything. It's disgusting."

"Get a hat on over that lump on your head. We'll put bananas over our mouths and noses . . . "

"A banana . . . on my nose."

"You know, like when we shovel grain, to keep the dust out."

"A bandana, you nitwit, not a banana."

"Yeah, whatever. Let's get started. Are you finished killing yourself with that cigarette yet?"

"Yeah, if you want to bite my banana, I'll be ready to go."

"Ha." André gives him a playful punch on the shoulder, then stretches his arms over his head.

Alice walks towards them trailing long-sleeved house-coats, leather gloves, and long scarves. "Here you are!" she calls. "Everything you need to keep the dust from your clothes and lungs. And these." From her apron pocket she pulls two pairs of welder's glasses, dark lenses with protective side shields. "They were Roland's." She hands them to her two brothers. "Put your glasses on, Maurice, safety first."

Maurice reaches out and perches the glasses on his nose. *I am too old for this shit.* "There," he says, "happy?" He stalks past them, wearing a lovely pink nylon housecoat.

"What's eating him?" asks Alice.

"Nothing. He is just a little tired today. The heat. You know he gets cranky in the heat and his leg is acting up." André crooks his arm towards Alice. "Madame, would you escort me? I believe we have a moth ball to attend."

Alice looks at her youngest brother with a ready smile, and then her gaze shifts. Hands on hips, she looks over the roofline, squinting. She brings one hand up to shade her eyes.

"André?"

"Yes?" He puts on his safety glasses and twists his head this way and that to see through the smears and the dust.

"André," she says, softer this time and no longer asking a question.

"Yes, I am." He still can't make out a damned thing. The glasses are so dark.

From inside the house they hear Maurice swinging the ball peen hammer into the ceiling. Thwuck. *"Enfant de Christ de tabernacle!"* Thwuck. *"Maudite bête d' l'enfer désespéré!"*

"André, there, do you see?" She puts her hand on his arm and leans towards the house.

Thwuck. "What the fu — ?"

A guttural ripping sound. The groan of a ceiling coming down mixed with the choked out bellow of a man caught under the debris. André and Alice run desperately for the house.

"Maurice? Maurice! Can you hear me?" calls André, waving one arm through the dust and wings and stench, keeping his other hand firmly clamped over the green nylon scarf that protects his mouth.

"Jésus-Marie-Joseph," breathes Alice. "Why would she do this?" She fans away the dust and surveys the boards, plaster, and wood chip insulation.

"Alice, stay over here by the kitchen door." André guides her back by the shoulder. "Call home. Get the kids over here quick as they can. Go!"

"I saw, just before the roof fell down, I saw . . . " begins Alice.

"Later, not now. I have to help Maurice. Call home and get them to come, now."

Tightening his jaw, he turns from his sister towards the living room. He sighs. There, near the corner where the TV used to be, is a humped crumpled figure. He crosses the living room in two strides and drops to his knees, already brushing the plaster and dust off Maurice. A swinging rafter has nicked his brother on the other side of his head. He removes a clean handkerchief from his pocket and applies pressure to the gash. Maurice groans thinly, and tries to open his eyes.

"Don't move, Maurice. I got you, *mon vieux*. I got you, you are okay. Took a bit of a hit to the head again, that's all. Maybe all of this'll knock some sense into you." He turns as far from his brother's ear as he can and yells to Alice, "Call Trefflés. He's bleeding like a pig from the head."

"No," croaks Maurice, "I just sweat like a pig."

"Yeah, well you bleed like one too," says André. He fumbles with Maurice's scarf, flaps it awkwardly to clean it and ties it around the handkerchief already stained with blood. "There, that should hold you. Does anything else hurt? Can you feel all your bones? Anything broken?" André clears the ceiling offal from around his brother.

"André, I fell. I fell off the ladder," says Maurice, eyes wide.

"I know you fell. Why the fuck were you doing it by yourself? Why didn't you wait for me? You could have waited you know, I was right behind you."

From the kitchen comes Alice's voice, "André?"

"Yes?"

"There was no answer at your place."

"The kids are on their way then."

"And I called the Chateau. Had to leave a message with the matron though. Madame Trefflé is sleeping they said. I told her to tell *La Vieille* that Maurice Garance was bleeding and to please stop it. Oh, there's the phone. I'll get it, it's probably for me anyway."

"André, I fell off the ladder before the ceiling fell," Maurice says.

"Yeah?"

"Something pushed me off the ladder. I was looking up into the attic. I had made a pretty good size hole and I felt something come down on top of my head and push me down, off the ladder. I fell before the ceiling did."

"It's your worse nightmare, Maurice. There must be at least a ton of moths here on the floor. That was what pushed you off the ladder and probably saved your life too. Acted liked a cushion, a big pillow, einh? Can you

26

feel that? Does that hurt? How about here, can you feel this?"

Alice pokes her head around the corner from the kitchen. "André?"

"Still here."

"Matron said she woke Émérentienne for the emergency. Has the bleeding stopped?"

"I'll check," He lifts one corner of the handkerchief. "Yes it has. Good. Thank you."

"You're welcome," she says and ducks back into the kitchen.

He hears her filling the kettle and lighting the stove. "I'll make some coffee now," she calls back.

"Tell her I need *l'eau forte*," says Maurice.

"Easy does it there. Can't have her and you both all screwy on the same day. Try standing up, einh?"

"I can stand. I tell you, André, I fell before the ceiling fell."

"Yes, yes, Maurice, all right, there. There you go. How does that feel? Are you okay to walk?"

"No goddammit, I think my ankle is fucked. Help me to a chair."

They both look up and around the bare room.

"It looks like a bomb went off in here," said Maurice. "A bomb of . . . what's that?"

"Remnants of a roof gone bad, where moths came to die," says André, shaking his head.

"No, I mean that, what is that?" Maurice points his chin towards a soft brown hump, half buried under the plaster.

"Looks like an old suitcase. God only knows what's in there. Probably extra Roland parts. We'll worry about that later. Come on. Let's get you to the kitchen."

The two brothers limp into the kitchen where Alice is fussing with the twenty-cup percolator. "Do you think this is enough? With the kids on the way I should probably make more, or maybe Kool-Aid. I used to have Kool-Aid."

Maurice drops heavily into a chair. "How about you break out a bottle? Do you have any honey wine left? Or some rye even? You always said alcohol was for emergencies. I could use a shot right about now."

Alice looks over at him. "I don't see why at every little thing you have to run to the bottle, Maurice."

"In case you haven't noticed, I am not exactly running anywhere."

"The pain in your ankle? That is a sprain. I can see from here it's not broken," she says.

"Oh for the love of Pete! I am asking you for one lousy cup of wine! Surely to God you can see . . . "

"Yes, I can see," says Alice. "I can see, that you have pain and Roland had pain and he became a small man, Maurice. Small enough to fit in a bottle and to never come out again."

"Alice, please. A drink."

André steps in. "All right you two, let it go. The kids will be here and I am not feeling so hot myself. The air isn't moving in here. Alice, I'm taking Maurice outside. You should come too."

He reaches under the sink, behind the potato bucket and pulls out a bottle of Five Star. The star hangs crookedly and Alice's spidery writing on the label reads, *Miel d'Autant*.

28

Maurice grins and opens his mouth to say something, but André shoots him a look to keep quiet. "Bring the glasses out would you please, Alice?" he says.

"Fine," she says. "I will bring two small glasses. And coffee."

They look out the window when they hear the crunch of tires on gravel. "Kids are here," says André. "They can help us with this mess. Alice? The glasses? Bring a few more, einh? The kids are going to love your famous honey wine. I think they'll need it. Then we'll get to work on the house."

Maurice is slow to rise. André slings one arm over his shoulder and one around his waist. They make wobbly progress to the stairs, where Maurice leans on the wall then steps down the three stairs into the yard.

Alice watches quietly. The kids, as André called them, close to or over six feet tall each and ranging between fourteen and eighteen years old, pile out of the car and stand still, peering through the living room windows.

André's youngest boy, Urbain, laughs when he sees the mess inside. "Wow! When you guys do a job, you really do the job!"

His brother, Pierre, comes up from the other side of the house. "Holy hell, Dad. What happened?"

"It was a little more far gone than we thought," says André.

"*Mon oncle* Maurice, you okay?" asks Léo, the eldest.

Maurice waves his hand, as though brushing away a fly. "Just a scratch," he says.

"Lucky it hit your head, eh?" laughs Léo.

"Yep, hit the second hardest part of me that's for sure." Maurice's voice tries to hide the throb in his head and the pain in his ankle. He feels all of his sixty-eight years, plus a hundred more.

"Hello, hello, les boys!" Alice arrives with a tray laden with cups, a pitcher of coffee, gingersnaps, and the Five Star bottle filled with mead. "What a nice surprise! Can you stay a while? I just made this little coffee party and here you all are."

"*Ma tante* Alice, did you do all this?" asks Léo. He takes the tray from his aunt and sets it down on an end table. The others circle him and pour coffee and mead into the mismatched cups.

"Don't be silly. We moved the furniture out here because your dad thought it would be easier to fix the roof that way. Then, I saw your mon oncle Maurice go in there and," she turns to the house, her voice drops, "I saw someone dancing on the roof," she finishes.

The young boys elbow each other and smile into their cups. Alice's gaze stays on the house and the copse of trees behind.

André however scowls, embarrassed at his sister's declaration. *They think she is a retard! I can see it in their faces.* "All right you ninnies," he says, "drink your coffee and let's get to work. There's been enough horseplay around here for one day."

Alice turns to him, her blue eyes searching his own. "You believe me, André. You know I saw someone dancing on the roof; you saw. You too, Maurice. Oh *non*, not you, because you were inside. You were knocked down off the ladder and landed with a suitcase on your head. Someone knocked you off the ladder." She pats Maurice on the arm. "I will be right back. Urbain, viens. I need your help."

30

Maurice struggles to say something to his sister, but she is already walking away, arm in arm with Urbain, towards the house. He wants to assure her, reassure her, help or at least comfort her somehow. She is becoming anxious and that is never a good sign. He looks to André. His mouth opens once then closes in frustration. He fumbles in his pocket for his kerchief and blows his nose. With the handkerchief he wipes a tear from his eye. *Damn dust and all.*

There is a pressure on his heart, like a hand is squeezing it. *Damnit! Am I having a heart attack?* He feels the hand squeeze again. It is a small brown hand, another sister's hand, his little Bella. Then her face before him, clear as a bell, as if no time has passed. He blows his nose again, long and loud, trying to expel the pressure somehow. He tucks the kerchief into his back pocket and walks painfully towards the house and the suitcase that slammed into him from more than fifty years ago.

What sang you here will bring you back.
— letters from Autant

AUTANT, 1952

Wednesday

ALICE GARANCE WAS THIRTEEN YEARS. In her bloomed the desire to shed childish ways, to take on the mannerisms of a woman. So instead of pinching her younger sister, Juliette, awake like she used to, Alice slipped from the bed they shared and quietly knelt at her side. She rocked back, keeping one eye closed, lips already mouthing the words. She pulled her rosary from the hand-me-down leather suitcase she kept under the bed. If she could say a hundred prayers today without speaking another word aloud, any wish would come true. She would pray to the Virgin Marie for a slice of her suffering patience, a woman's flimsy shield against evil.

It was something her grandfather had taught her and usually this only worked on Good Friday, but Alice had been trying to win the attention of Adrien Trefflé for almost eight months now. Adrien had been hired to help build a new outbuilding, a shed for tools.

Yesterday, as Alice hoed the garden, he had given her a lock made of wood, a simple yet intricate puzzle of carpentry. "You could put it on your jewellery box. To keep your jewels safe," he said.

He stepped toward her then, his hand reaching without guile to touch her gold cross pendant. They had moved closer, close enough to kiss. But he had backed away again when Papa rounded the corner of the house. Edgar Garance was intrigued with the warded lock and marvelled at the craftsmanship.

"How'd you get in there? This is a tiny thing, not more than what? Six inches by five inches?

"I borrowed *Pépère*'s scroll tools to start and finished the rest with a knife. It's pretty small but it works."

"Is this pine? That can't be easy to cut . . . "

Together they walked away, talking about smoothing shackles, key inserts, wax, and how to cut proper notches on dowels.

She had touched him six times already. Twice on their way into church, just the back of his coat but still, that counted. Once on the arm at Toupin's store, right at the counter with Madame Toupin looking and everything; and once between the stacks of material and the cheese wheel; also at the store when he bumped into her, his arms laden with groceries. He'd said, "Excuse me, *désolé*," and had smiled. That counted for almost two touches really, the bumping into and the smile.

And once, once they sat next to each other just outside the Post Office and she had touched his leg. This was thanks to his *mémère* squishing them together as she squeezed herself onto the small bench. Then, of all the rotten luck, Mémère badgered him to go check on his pépère Baptist's progress at the garage. Alice had definitely felt his thigh lift from hers. He turned to her, grinned, touched the brim of his cap and said, "Goodbye, Alice. Be right back, Mémère."

Madame Trefflé had practically pushed Alice off the seat at that point, settling her fat self more completely, as if she meant to take root on that bench. But who could begrudge a visiting grandmother her place on the bench?

So, six touches and he had given her that lovely little wooden lock the other day. Alice checked her suitcase. Yes, there it was, safe and sound. She felt around the satin lining again and pulled out a small hand mirror. She brought the mirror closer to her face, letting the sun highlight her profile, first one side then the other. Her skin was clear and pale. Eyes grey-blue. Hair, long, honey coloured and shiny, thanks to the vinegar rinses and cold water. Her mouth was thin-lipped, rosy — could it be pouty?

"What are you doing? Are you eating a pickle? Mom will kill you if you have food up here." Juliette leaned over the side of the bed. "Where did you get the mirror, Alice? Can I see it?"

"No, Juliette, you may not," said Alice.

"Why?" asked Juliette.

"Ma tante Léah gave it to me."

"But, why? When did she give it to you? What for?" Juliette knelt on the mattress, hands on hips, gearing for a fight.

"Because I am the oldest and I am a woman, that's why. A woman needs a mirror," said Alice. With a snap, the treasures were safe inside the case and pushed under the bed. She sighed what she thought was an appropriate sigh for woman in such a situation and got up off her knees. She began dressing for the day.

"You? A woman? Stinky fart's more like it," said Juliette. She flipped her long red hair up over her face, covering her dark blue eyes. Her body was taut, quivering like a bow strung a little too tight. She was shorter than

Alice and all the more stubborn for it. Three years and a natural misunderstanding separated them.

"I know you are, but what am I?"

"*Les filles?* Rise and shine!" Their mother poked her head up through the opening in the floor. "All of you, time to get up. The garden needs watering and we need more cattails for the baskets. We're having company for supper, so the house needs a good going over as well. It's going to be a hot one today, so the quicker we can get things done, the better."

"Are Trefflés coming?" Bella asked.

Bella had been awake the whole time. She shared the blue eyes of her sisters, but the similarities ended there. Bella had dark hair, her mother's pride and bane because it was so thick and curly it usually ended up in two fat pigtails or one stubby ponytail.

"Why in God's name would I invite Trefflés?"

"I heard Alice talking. You were talking in your head about Adrien Trefflé, right? I heard you say his name. You like him, right? Wouldn't it be nice to have him over for supper?"

"Toupins are coming," Lucille said, now all the way upstairs, bending when she got to the end of the room because the roof came down in the corners. It was early morning and already stifling up there. She pretended she hadn't heard Bella's comment about reading Alice's thoughts. Lucille did that a lot lately, to discourage Bella from telling people what she could see inside their heads. Not to mention visits she had from the spirits and spooks. No need to ask whether or not the nuns at school would appreciate the "little reports" Bella felt free to give, once she started school in September.

36

"Toupins? Oh non, Mom, not them!" said Juliette. Her high-pitched voice cut through the clamour of Maurice being rousted from the nest he called a bed.

"Juliette, enough."

Alice ignored all of them and pulled her nightdress over her head. She made a show of properly folding and placing it on the small stool beside the bed.

Maurice's tawny head poked up from the dishevelled blankets. He still sported the baby fat of childhood around his middle but his arms and legs were strong and tanned from a couple months of summer. He grabbed his pillow and threw it at Alice. "Hey, chicken-butt lips!"

"Maurice, stop. Why say such a thing to your sister? Such language." Lucille worked a T-shirt over his head.

"Maybe Trefflés will come some other day, Alice," Bella said.

" . . . and *Mademoiselle* Chicken-Butt Lips will get a chance to kiss her frog!" Juliette whispered to Maurice as she dropped the pillow on his head. Maurice screwed up his face and made kissing noises.

"Oh enough, Juliette. Maurice, *c'est assez. Dépêche-toi.* Don't tease your sister like that. Get a move on." Lucille's voice was stern and the firmness added just enough menace to let them know that they were done here.

Edgar's voice rang up the stairs and froze them all in place, *"Les enfants, c'est assez."*

Lucille looked at Alice. Alice looked menacingly over at Juliette and Maurice, who grinned back.

"Yes, enough," Lucille said. She smiled at them, and ruffled Maurice's hair. "Fine. Now, everyone make your beds. Bella, hurry up, *puce*, get dressed."

Downstairs, she made apologies for the children. "This heat is getting to them. Work outside today will help slough off that extra energy. I wish they would put that energy in a bottle and give me some. Must be a full moon coming or a storm."

Edgar said, "And I, I have had enough with shaving. I don't think I need to shave today. I'm already pretty damned good looking. Don't you think?" He turned to his wife.

"Shave. Good looking or no," she said. "What will Florence think when she comes over for supper and you even have a hint of beard? Sloth and slovenly, that's what she'll think. And don't think she is above sharing that opinion with everyone and anyone, at any time, anywhere."

"She'll say, 'Now that is one hairy chicken butt!' Bah! I don't give two cents for what Florence Toupin says," said Edgar.

"Edgar! Honestly. You are worse than the kids. And you wonder were they get it from."

"I don't wonder, ma vieille, I know. Their dear mother has such a tongue on her . . . "

"Me?" She reached across the table for him, but he dodged her fingertips and made for the door, grinning.

"I am going out to the shop for a bit," he said. "When your brother comes by, tell him I'm back there."

"Joseph? What does he want?"

"Just might come by is all."

"Invite him for supper. Edgar? Edgar, do you hear me? And tell him to bring Léah."

She turned from the sideboard where she had been slicing bread. Edgar was already outside, screen door banging shut behind him.

"Mom? Alice is being mean again." Juliette stood at the foot of the stairs, tear-stained face, braid in disarray, holding Bella's hand.

"What is wrong with you all today? Am I the only sane one left in this house? Upstairs and get dressed, Juliette. Bella, you too. Oh, you are dressed. Good girl, help me by setting the table. Juliette, go get dressed."

Alice poked her head through the hole in the ceiling, "Mom, whatever she is saying, she's lying."

Bella asked, "Mom? Am I? Am I a sane one?" In a family with so many children, Bella found it was usually best to check. Her right eye was tearing. A small knot of pain was forming in her head. She blinked.

Lucille looked at her and hesitated one heartbeat too long. "Of course you are sane, Belle Bella, of course. And a good little helper too. Now, go get the butter from the fridge. The door is sticky, so pull hard. Get the honey too, if you can reach it."

"I don't need help," Bella said. "I am a good helper. I can bring the jar down."

Alice came down the stairs, dignity restored. Lucille watched as she checked her reflection in the small window along the wall, licking her finger and smoothing her eyebrows, smiling.

"Why can't you smile at your sister like that?" Lucille asked.

Alice turned and Lucille could still see her little girl with short uneven braids, barely visible, but still there in the wide blue eyes.

"Oh, Mom."

"Alice, you are a lovely girl. Try to act like one."

"It's not my fault! Juliette, she . . . "

"Ah, non." Lucille held her daughter in place with the look that reminded Alice of being caught in a prickly bush, unable to move for fear of scratching skin to blood. "Remember, an ugly tongue cuts twice. First, the person you insult gets hurt and then you hurt yourself, poison yourself with hateful words. Get along with Juliette. Be a lady, and you can start by . . . "

A lady. Mom called me a lady! From now on I am a lady . . . I will . . . Alice walked in a daze to the cupboard, one hand out. She touched the bread. Everything her mother said was lost to her. Something about tongues, poison, and she thought she heard bees. Her other hand reached for the knife.

" . . . toasting the bread. Alice? Did you hear me? Toast some bread for the others. And shut your mouth before the bees get in."

Bella moved quietly. She brought the honey jar to the table. She slid the butter closer to Alice and picked up the bread knife.

Glint of silver through sunlight. Bella tipped the knife blade. It sliced light into her eyes. It made sparkles behind her eyelids and made the headache go away for a second. She tipped it away. The headache came back, quietly pinching her brain until she felt a little sick. She waited until Alice drifted from the table to the bathroom, then she crept under the table and hunched there. She angled the blade, lit her mother's shoe. Rode the shoe to the sink, to the table, to the cupboard, to the sink. Her mother stood, hands on the edge of the counter. She looked out the window over the sink. She blocked the sun.

Bella waited under the table, hardly breathing, head throbbing, and all she wanted was to continue the game. She wanted the sun to come out.

Her mother leaned forward, letting the light warm the top of her head. Smoke wisped from her crown, slipped down her shoulders. She was burning out strange thoughts, black moths she called them, by facing the sun, by absorbing light. There was a soft kick at the door and Joseph came into the kitchen.

"I got a need for your strong coffee, 'cille," he said. "My head."

He lowered himself onto a chair at the table. Bella scooted out from underneath and stood shyly by the pantry door, a little dizzy.

"And a good morning to you too, Brother. Is this the only reason you came this morning? To beg coffee?" said Lucille.

"Coffee . . . " he moaned, putting his face in his hands.

"Does your head hurt too, mon oncle Joseph?" asked Bella. She inched closer to the table on tiptoes, avoiding the red stars on the linoleum.

He looked at her from between his fingers. Bella made the light glint from the knife blade onto the tabletop and skated it up towards his arms.

"You cannot burn this out, girl. You should, cut, it, out!" He laughed and made a half-hearted lunge for the knife.

Bella giggled and swayed away from him.

Eyeing her brother, Lucille could smell the migraine on him.

"You could use a hot bath," she said. "Go pick a ribbon, Bella. I will braid you a good one before you go play outside. Your hair is getting so long." She held her hand out for the knife.

The girl slipped past her uncle, passing her mom the shiny blade. She pirouetted in front of the blue kitchen door and patted it. She sang, as much to the door as to her mother, "I love you, big as the big blue-sky bowl, big as the ocean, forever."

"Go already," her mother said, brandishing the knife, "before I skin you like a coyote!"

Singing softly, Bella disappeared into her parents' bedroom. "Today, today, a red ribbon day. Long hair for me, yeah headache headache go away."

Lucille shook her head and reached for two cups from the shelf. She poured coffee and sat facing her brother.

"Honey?"

"Yes, darling?"

She tapped her finger against his cup. "Idiot. Do you want honey?"

"Of course, yes, please."

She pushed the jar over to him.

Joseph wrapped his hand around the container. "Spoon," he rasped.

"Right here," she rattled the jar full of spoons in the centre of the table.

He put a spoon into the near-empty jar, it rattled against the sides. He winced at the noise. "Dry. Nothing left in here but toast crumbs and spit," he muttered.

"There's always more honey," she said. Going into the pantry she pulled the plastic pail from the shelf and thunked it down at his feet. Joseph jumped. "What in hell, Joseph? Why does the big head sit on you?"

"Toupin. Figures I stole lumber from Massie's load. Says I'll lose my job. Shithead."

"Why does he think it was you?"

"Because I was the last to leave the yard. Tied the load down myself. Was responsible for it, he says. Shithead. Like I don't know that."

"Joseph, did you?"

"What the fuck do I need lumber for?"

"You want to build a place for you and Léah."

"Chicken coop suits me fine."

"That old shed isn't good for a married couple, even if you did insulate it."

"I am no thief, Lucille. You know that. I am lots of things, but I'm no thief."

"What about Nigger?"

"Dog followed me home is all. Can't help that Léah fed it and it stayed around."

"Joseph, if . . . "

"If, nothing! My own sister thinks I am a thief. Well no thank you," he growled. "Your coffee is bitter this morning." He pushed back his chair. "It makes me sick."

"Oh come on. Joseph, please, I don't mean . . . " She rose and followed him.

He shrugged her off.

"Take a bath. Come for supper tonight and bring Léah," she said.

He didn't answer, just walked through the door, across the porch and down the stairs. Lucille sat back in her chair. She turned her mug by the handle three times then raised it to drink.

"Mom?" Bella held ribbon and brush in her hand.

Her mother smiled and motioned her to a chair.

"Did mon oncle Joseph give you his headache?" she asked, eyes following the throb at her mother's temple.

"Non, *chouette*," Lucille said. She rose and slowly brushed her daughter's long black hair. "This one is mine, all mine."

"Do you want me to cut, it, out?" Bella playfully mimed cutting with scissors.

"I want you, to sit." Her mother reined her in, gently pulling her hair. "Just sit still. I need to pray your braid and I need you to pray with me."

Each twist of hair, each over-under connection, was blessed. *"Je vous salue Marie, pleine de grâce . . . "* began Bella. Lucille mouthed words in a different language to appease a somewhat different god, the one who had created her world. She had the feeling to protect her daughter from the mischief that was coming.

Prayer finished, kiss delivered on the back of her neck, Bella slipped out the door and shadowed her uncle to the shoe repair shop just behind the house. Three soft toe raps on the bottom of the door frame and he pushed open the door. "Hey," said Joseph.

"Hey, good to see you, *bonhomme*. Bella, go help your mom," said Edgar, looking around Joseph. Bella said nothing, already preoccupied with the pile of leather scraps, looking for a perfect piece. She loved the smell and the feel of leather.

Joseph reached over and stroked her head. "Hey, fille," he said softly, "go on, eh, get lost. We don't need no women hearing our business."

Bella looked up at her uncle, patted his hand and left the shop. A small patch of leather tucked into her pants pocket, for later.

Joseph sighed, slouching over to the counter that divided the shop in two.

Edgar smoothed the sole of the boot he was working on with glue, and slowly lowered it to cover the upturned bottom of the boot. He studied the arrangement, made a small adjustment and, satisfied, pressed down on the new piece with the flat of his hand.

"*Proche comme ça c'est un beau mariage.* 'What I put together let no man take apart.' Someone smart said that."

"Yes, yes, everything stays together until it all comes flying apart," said Joseph.

"Yes, time has the persistence to undo things. That's why God made glue," Edgar answered. Without so much as a glance, he picked up his pipe from the ashtray set amongst tiny tin trays filled with various-sized nails. "So?" He gave his brother-in-law time to answer, gently scraping out the bowl of his pipe with the point of leather-cutting shears.

"So," sighed Joseph, propping his chin on his hands. He gazed mournfully at the glue jar.

"And?" Edgar tamped tobacco down and lit it, cheeks hollowed to draw in the smoke.

"And so, I wonder why everyone hates me so much," Joseph said. He picked at the encrusted jar.

"Not everyone hates you. I think Léah and that dog of yours must love you, seeing as how they haven't left yet," said Edgar. "And Bella, she listens to you."

"Hmm?" Joseph looked intently at the gob between his fingers. The glue had warmed and was slowly regaining its natural elasticity.

"Playing with that will give you sticky fingers."

"Einh? What? Why do you say that? Look I never took nothing, I swear! Damned Toupin has no right!" He slammed his fist on the counter, spraying a tray of tacks.

"Whoa there! Whoa!" Edgar leaned forward and righted the glue pot. "I'm riding a blind horse here. Slow down and come again."

"Toupin said I took half of the lumber from Massie's wagonload night before last. I never was even near the mill, I swear. He said I could even lose my job at the Post Office. I can't be trusted! Called in the bastard-village-council guys and everything. Snooping around, buggering about. They could have found, you know, stuff." Joseph looked up carefully from the rescued tray of tacks. "You know?"

"Yes, I know. Don't worry about Toupin. He came over yesterday. I'm part of the bastard-council too, remember. We went over to the yard and looked around where the lumber was stacked on those pallets. Footprints mostly washed out because of the rain."

Joseph slumped.

"But, we were lucky with that rain too, because a couple of footprints were as clear as a bell. Must have been where the thief stood with some lumber in his arms or something heavy like that, waiting for a truck. He stood there, under the overhang, while he loaded the lumber. Those prints were deep."

Joseph turned and gripped the counter, lifted his eyebrows. "And?"

46

"They don't belong to you."

"Of course they don't belong to me, I told Toupin that. I told him, 'You . . .' Bah! Who was it then? Can you tell who the footprints belong to?"

"Ah well, now wait, did the council members find any 'stuff' at your place?"

"Non, non, they think they know everything, but they don't. And, they think they look everywhere, but they don't." Joseph winked and leaned his elbows on the counter. "Tell me."

"Tonight, how about you bring what we have bottled as far as Marie Reine? Keep a few bottles for *la Fête*. Hide the rest in the cache until we're ready for a little boat ride later on this summer. I have a proposition for Toupin regarding the honey. And what with *la Fête au Village*, he won't be out investigating anything until next week."

"What do you mean, a proposition? You going to cut him in?" said Joseph.

"Non, non. No need to make this a village enterprise, einh? It's just us, me and you. Can you make it to the river?"

"Yes. But, I could sure use a trip up to Peace River. Get away from this place for a while. You want I should go all the way then?"

"No, it would be too easy to think you were guilty if you ran away. La Reine is far enough, I can call over and make sure someone takes the load up farther. It's only a dozen or so jars. We can't get greedy now. Plus, I feel a little uneasy with this thief about."

"Ah yes, the thief. So who is it then? It would be easy for you to figure that out, Shoemaker Man." Joseph smiled and picked up fallen nails with the sticky part of his fingers. "Hector Toupin is clever, coming to you for help. Oh yes, Autant is full of clever men."

"I told him I'd have to come back here and check the boots and shoes I have in the shop, you see, to make sure. It wouldn't be right to accuse a man of a crime without adequate proof," said Edgar. He scooped up the last of the nails that Joseph had tipped over and swept them back into the tray.

"Sure sure, and?"

"Well now. I can't say exactly. Just that some people," he said pointing to the boot in front of him, "wear down the sole where the ball of their big toe rests. And, I had another visitor who was interested in those tracks."

"Who?"

"Philip Trefflé. Came by to offer a pig for la Fête au Village last night. We got to talking about things and the missing lumber came up."

"Bullshit! Philip Trefflé offered you a pig? That bastard wouldn't offer you the jam between his toes unless . . . oh. Yeah, sure."

"Thief won't be found unless he wants to be found. Maybe it was those from the reserve. I'll suggest to Constable Toupin that he check there. See if any new shacks are going up."

"Jésus, you are a smart old shoemaker man, Edgar Garance!"

"I just watch and listen, Joseph Corneille. I watch and listen."

Lucille was fretful, anxious; she hadn't told anyone, but she hadn't gone to the bathroom in four days. This constipation was torture. It was obvious something wasn't working properly, the sharp lines radiating from the middle of her tongue said as much. Her jaw stayed as clenched as her hands as the band of pain netted along her temples and in her tortured gut. She was loath to ask la vieille Trefflé for help. Her worry had to do with Bella's increasing headaches, yes that, but more, there was something more.

It had started with finding the outline of faces in stones, in sweat stains on clothing, in leaves, and how they shadowed bark. Some said that seeing these faces, angels in this disguise, was a blessing. They came to let people know that someone was watching.

Then, the sound of bees, a long, slow droning. Bees while she stood still and while she hung the wash outside. Low insistent throbs, the number eight on its side.

Finally, there were dreams of hot pressing things, fingers, hands, pulling and pushing at her. The top of her head was touched over and over again, leaving a creepy-crawling feeling. Lucille knew that soon she would see what had been hidden. What people were thinking would complete itself in her mouth. She would answer before being called, bring what was not yet desired. Someone had been praying and they were still so busy praying, that they didn't hear or see the signs they had given. She received them instead. *Bella is probably feeling the same way*, she thought. *I saw her eye was twitchy at breakfast.*

She walked heavily to the front door and leaned against the doorframe. Smells crowded up against her back from inside the house, lye soap, this morning's coffee and toast. Home smells, good real smells; but not strong enough to mask the odour her brother had brought with him into the house this morning. If anything, it seemed to get stronger after he left. What was this mischief going to shape into? *I pray it is not for my Bella. If she starts bleeding, only Émérentienne Trefflé can stop the bleeding now. What good am I? I can't even help my own daughter.*

There was a low rumbling from the north. She looked up, scratched the inside of her wrist, and wrinkled her nose. There was that gunmetal smell, like before rain or snow. Thunder?

She scratched absently at the kitchen door. Tracing with strong, thin fingers the ship she had drawn there under the layers of blue paint. The ship she had seen in her dreams, a tall sailing ship. She heard its sails unfurl and snap as the sheets on the line at the back of the house. Chains thundered up, along planks from bow to stern, fore to aft, iron rubbing against wood and groaning as the ship ploughed through water. She loved that ship, and this door was blue to be both the water below the ship and the sky above it. It was a haven between worlds.

Lucille fingered the necklace at her throat, one side blue glass beads, the other every other colour she had. At its centre was a black, heart-shaped stone pierced through by a smaller stone. She had found the stone when she was a girl. The stone called to her and she picked it up. Careful to rinse it in her mouth so it would always know her and would never stray. In return, the stone gave her dreams of a tall ship, a beautiful woman with blue eyes, long red hair and, then, a small boat on dark water.

Edgar thought she was beautiful, although her father had said that the best part of her was when she was walking away because he said he didn't have to see her ugly face. Who would believe that Monsieur Edgar Garance would love her? Deformed and a Corneille to boot.

50

A bee lit on the door. Lucille put her finger near the little jewelled sac of pollen on the back leg. The bee turned around and climbed onto her finger. She brought it to her face and closed her eyes, allowing the bee to travel her skin, absorbing the heat and the story she had come to collect.

Lucille felt clawed feet running messages along her lips, knew the bee was hard at work tracing paths and memorizing mouth lines, coding where the honey had been this morning. Now the bee walked to her eyes and circled over the fine hairs, gauging salt, moisture' and heat. Lucille's skin stretched and memory moved through antennae.

This one was born with the hole in her mouth, on the roof. They say a candle in a church is a thing of beauty. A candle in the wilderness though, now that is a miracle. This one is that kind of candle; delivered into a world where she could not be expected to survive. But she did.

Her mother had knelt with the baby in her arms on the steps of the church, not invited in of course. By the borrowed light of the sacristy candle above the altar, she had prayed to The Mother. She heard a voice, soft and low, instructing her to pull out the bottom jaw, to keep the throat clear. She dreamed to feed her baby slowly, only a trickle at a time. Feed her through a small, wet rawhide tube poked right down the throat.

Tricky business that, being fed as a bird for almost a whole year. The hole finally webbed over and the only damage was that the baby's chin stayed a little small.

The bee climbed down the bridge of her nose, carefully tucking the story into the sacs on her back legs. She flew off. A magpie landed on the roof of the house without making a sound. It had no shadow.

Lucille came to herself with a start. She brushed at her face as though a spider web clung there. She glanced up across the yard. Sunlight glaring, shadows thin as the edge of a knife, it was noon. She had to get lunch out to the men.

She gathered what she needed for a quick meal. Jellied beef tongue sandwiches, a couple pickled beets for colour, radishes from the garden, and two jars of tea, brewed in the sun. She rummaged the pantry for the biscuits she had made for last night's supper. The plate was decidedly lighter. Maurice and Bella must have stuffed their pockets before leaving for the creek. *Good, they will have something to eat along the way.* She ran her hand along the shelf for the honey. When her fingers felt a sticky spot, she remembered it was in the kitchen. She pulled down a jar of beets and a small black stone clattered to the floor. Bella and her stash of presents. The girl left stones for her inside shoes, beside the bed, under the pillow. It was her way of saying I love you, goodbye, and I took four biscuits this morning.

Lucille brought the little stone to her lips and kissed it before slipping it into her front pocket. *I will have to give this shelf a good scrubbing before putting anything else in here.*

She put the food in a wooden box and covered it with a piece of oilcloth.

PHILIP TREFFLÉ WAS VERY HAPPY. By tomorrow morning, the new room would be up, no one the wiser. He would finally have his wife off his back. He would have the lumber gone and at least one of the sickly pigs too. Gone to Edgar's and off his mind. *Edgar Garance will be in my debt for the village-party pig. It is a debt I can collect in honey-whiskey by fall. God is showing His good side to me because I am a careful planner, a wise man.*

He watched his wife move through the kitchen, setting water to boil, bending over the wood box for small sticks and scraps of bark to start a fire in the stove. Émérentienne had been a fine looking girl at sixteen, when he married her. Now, after having squeezed out three runt daughters and four sons she was a hag. She was still a hard worker though and those little bastards worked as hard as he made them work, with the toe end of his boot or by the ball of his fist. They would grow up knowing that this land would give only what was forced from it. Everything here was a test of will, of brute strength.

He yanked on his boots, stamped down hard on the heel, making the floorboards ring. *Now, it is time to work. Adrien needs to work here today, and I'll get Corneille. Get that lumber sorted out and the walls done at least. Then see about a pig. Feels like blood today!*

Émérentienne shivered. She heard him bang around behind the wall that marked their room from the rest

53

of the house. Feeding kindling to the glowing coals in the stomach of the stove, she took a minute to pray. She prayed that the clothes wouldn't get blown from the line, that her children would be safe and that Philip would take one day from the drink. *What kind of ramencheur am I if I can't even help my own husband?*

She didn't open her eyes when she sensed him walking behind her. It was twenty steps, twenty to the door. *Let him make it to the door. Let him not stop for the bottle.* Thirteen, fourteen, fifteen, sixteen, seventeen. He stopped. He was beside the cupboard. He snapped his suspenders. Eighteen, nineteen. He stopped.

"Call over to Garance. Get the boy back. We need him here today," he said.

She heard the creak of the door, twenty. Out the door. She rose stiffly. *Merci.* She touched the stove front to make a cross there, then crossed herself quickly. A miracle. *Today, anything is possible.* Carefully, she lifted the receiver on the phone and politely asked the operator to call Edgar Garance.

Outside, Philip fumbled his penis from beneath woollen pants and grunted in satisfaction as urine splashed his wife's flowerbed, there beside the door. He laughed. An ugly sound that caused the scrawny dog to back away even farther under the lilac bush. Philip grunted again, tucking himself in. He whistled for the dog to come. There was purpose to his day.

The dog rose to his feet. Neck and legs tensed, a low growl rumbled from his chest. He shot through the lilac hedge, barking. Philip could hear shouts and screams from beyond there, and he smiled. *That'll teach the little buggers to go sneaking around. That'll teach them manners.*

"WHERE'S BELLA?" ASKED ALICE. SHE was back from the house. A lady does not pee outside.

Juliette thought it was a big waste of time, a way of getting out of doing the weeding. "At the creek," she said. "Mom told Maurice to get more reeds and Bella went with him."

"Mom thinks she needs her hat. Have they been gone long?"

"No, not long." Juliette stood, stretching her arms over her head.

"Let's go find them. Mom said she was getting a headache and she knows she's supposed to wear her hat."

"She hates that fucking thing," said Juliette. "It makes her feel retarded."

"You told her she looked retarded. Anyway, we can finish and rake the rest of the weeds later and, I bet you could use a walk in the creek right now." Alice smeared the sweat on Juliette's arm.

Juliette braced herself for a pinch or a slap in that almost tender gesture. When none came, she looked at her sister, warily. *The sun has fried her brain.*

Alice reached for her hand. To hold hands like when they were kids. To stay together and watch out for each other, like Mom asked them, to be together without fighting.

"Just a second," said Juliette. She pulled her hand back. "I think I have a splinter from the damned hoe."

"Do you always have to swear like a lumberjack?"

"No, Miss Priss. Sometimes I swear like a trucker."

"Ugh, you're disgusting."

"I can swear like mon oncle Joseph and use all the church words at one go."

"You're quite disgusting. You know that?"

"I know you are, but what am I?"

From the direction of the creek came a wail, like a coyote, but it was too early in the day for coyotes, wasn't it?

"What the . . . ?" Alice turned. "Is that Maurice?"

Another wail, then silence.

"Come on!" Alice jerked around and flew through the garden.

"Shit-hell, fuck-damn!" said Juliette. She dropped the hoe and ran towards the creek.

Bella was fanning the reeds to dry in the sun. The sun was too bright. She clenched her jaw to keep from throwing up. Her mom's biscuit had done nothing to soothe her nausea. A dry piece of bread or a pickle sometimes helped when she felt a headache, but the biscuit was too rich, too fresh. She closed her eyes. There was no shade, no resting place here, just noise and light. She had to turn the light off somehow. The thunder rumbled through her stomach. She was thirsty, so she took the small piece of leather from her pocket and sucked on it to make saliva in her mouth.

Maurice crowed like a rooster every time he grabbed and cut a cattail. "Now this is the way to cut reeds," he said importantly. "First, you grab them here, and, ungh! you cut like, ugnh! this and this and this, ugnh!"

The cattail sprang free and Maurice landed backwards, up to his neck in murky creek water. He struggled to his feet, coughing. He turned to shore, but the mud sucked at his calves. He threw the cattail in Bella's direction. "Here, la vieille, catch!" he said.

Bella stretched over the edge of the creek bank. Put one hand in the bush nearest her and leaned towards the floating cattail. She pushed the edge of the leather piece into her mouth so it wouldn't get wet or lost. Maurice was bellowing a song now, hacking with a vengeance. Three more cattails floated towards her. She wanted to help. The headache made her dizzy. She crammed the leather into her cheek and hunched down to reach the reed.

The bank wasn't more than rotting vegetation and clay. She slipped into the water with a muffled yelp. The red willow bush she was holding snapped back. She slapped at the water. Maurice had his back to her.

"Come on, ma vieille, that's the way! We'll have this forest cleared before sunset and we'll build the barn tonight!" he sang.

Bella raised her face above the surface, struggled to breathe and struggled for a foothold. The leather slid to the back of her mouth. She opened her mouth and water rushed in. She couldn't stand in this confusion of reeds, rocks and muck; she couldn't see. Her eyes bulged. Her head went down again.

"What are you doing?" yelled Maurice, finally looking back over his shoulder. "You'll scare away the

57

f-i-s-s-s-sh! Bella? Non! Hang on! Hang on, I'm coming, I'm com . . . " He whirled around and lurched one step at a time towards his sister. Towards the red shirt, there now, there now, almost, one more step. He threw himself the last distance separating them. He grabbed at her waist, his hands flailing muck and water high into the air. He heaved and they both fell farther into the creek. He struggled for breath and a firmer hold. "Don't be dead, Bella," he moaned through his own snot. "Don't be dead! Come on! Come on, help me! Help me!" He struggled with the sudden pig-heavy weight of his little sister. "I can't lift you. Help!"

"Maurice!" screamed Alice. She ploughed toward them, slipping and jerking to a sudden stop as the muck pulled at her. She heaved Bella upwards by the braid, her face skimming the surface, up and out of Maurice's grip.

Juliette plunged into the water beside Alice. She wrapped her arms around Bella's waist, slammed her on her own slight hip and turned back to the bank. It was as though Bella weighed nothing. There was no room for mistakes in this place. She had her dad's set look, like when he was opening up a hive.

Alice clutched at Maurice. She shook him. "What happened? What happened? What did you do?"

His hands came up to protect his face. "Bella she, she fell and I tried to help, she was so heavy. I tried."

Alice slumped and her hands fell from his shoulders. She lifted her arm. Maurice waited for the slap, he covered his face, sobbing. She pushed the hair from his forehead and pulled him to her. They half-walked, half-dragged each other to the bank.

Juliette pressed on Bella's stomach. She rolled her over on her side and a stream of water trickled out. She prised open her mouth and snaked thin fingers into the back of Bella's throat. A little way down, felt a slimy piece of something. Slowly curling her fingers, she pulled, afraid that whatever was in there would break in half. She hardly glanced at the material once it was free before snapping it to the side and angling herself behind Bella. Propping her up would keep her from swallowing her own vomit.

Bella's head bobbed as Juliette jiggled her. Suddenly she strained upwards. She threw up what water was in her and took a shuddering breath.

"Maurice?" Alice said to his huddled figure.

Maurice hunched lower, head turned in his arms. He didn't speak. Everything he said would be wrong. When people really listened to him, waited for his answer, it was always wrong.

She grabbed his arm and hauled him to stand. Eyes lowered, he said softly, "Sorry Alice. I lost your knife."

"My? You took my knife? You lost it? Stupid little turd," she spluttered. Alice shook her head. *Idiot! Crazy as a loon that one. He is worried about losing my knife? He . . . he . . . he should be glad that's all that was lost today.* The realization stunned her. "Stupid, stupid turd. Find it, Maurice," she said. "You are responsible."

Bella whimpered. Her legs and arms twitched. Juliette curled over her, humming and rocking her gently. Alice knelt down and felt Bella's face. She listened to her chest. Satisfied with the rhythm and inner gurglings, she stood her up. "We need to get home," she said. "Juliette, I'll carry her a while, then you."

Juliette sniffed back tears. She wiped them angrily away when she saw Alice looking at her. "Screw you, I'll carry her," she said.

Alice seemed not to have heard. She hoisted Bella higher onto her hip and started up the hill towards the house.

They walked and carefully juggled Bella between them. They were all dripping wet. Maurice, trudging behind, yelped when a magpie landed between him and his sisters. "Now what?" snapped Alice. There was blood under Bella's nose and Juliette absently wiped at it with her shirtsleeve. Alice scolded her; blood is tough to get out without cold water. Bella coughed, and spit blood.

"No, no nononononon." Maurice knew this was bad. He knew that when Bella started bleeding sometimes she couldn't stop. "What will we do?' he moaned.

"Oh shit, oh shit, oh Bella, no. Hang on, hang on," whispered Juliette. "We need help. Madame Trefflé, and we need Mom, go get Mom, Maurice."

Alice was shaking. "We'll go to Trefflés, meet us there," she said. She gripped Bella tighter and started for Trefflé's yard. "Run!"

Before Maurice could even turn around, Trefflé's dog, Bête, came hurtling towards them. Snarling, he honed in on the group now huddled together. Juliette kicked out. "Nasty Bête! Bad dog! Get lost! No Bête, no! Leave us alone, asshole! Maurice, stay here. Bête, you shithead, Maurice, don't run. We will go together. Bête bad dog, bad dog. I hate you!"

The children were at the lilac bushes now and pushed their way through the pointy grabby whippy branches.

Alice stumbled up the stairs to the porch calling, "Madame! Madame, help. It's Bella. Bella needs help!"

Émérentienne opened the screen door wide and they nearly fell in. "On the table, it's clean. Up, up, come on hurry!" she said. They lay Bella down and Émérentienne removed the girl's shoes and socks. She ordered Juliette to get a bowl of water and dishtowels from the drawer. She told Alice to clean her up. "If your Maman sees her like this, she'll have a heart attack." Madame made the sign of the cross on Bella's forehead and her heart. Raising each leg in turn, she slapped Bella on the soles of her feet. She held her hand in her own, closed her eyes and began to pray.

Alice wiped down her sister's face and arms. When she turned to rinse the cloth, she saw the phone. Why hadn't she thought of it before? "Juliette," she whispered, "call Mom." Juliette stared at her sister. Kids didn't use the phone, especially not neighbours' phones, and most especially not Trefflé's. Alice looked at Madame Trefflé, deep in prayer; she looked outside, no one in the yard. "It's for Bella. It's okay."

Juliette dragged her feet to the black phone on the wall. She lifted the receiver and waited to hear the click of the operator then told Mrs. Mullen who she was, and to please connect her to her mom. Mrs. Mullen snapped that she had already connected this party line with the Garance house once today and that was enough. She, after all, was not in the employ of Lucille Garance. She had other people who also desperately needed to contact other people. Juliette gritted her teeth and told her it was an emergency. It was for Bella. She heard the phone ringing in their house.

"HEY, *LA VIEILLE*! WHATCHA GOT there? Presents?" Edgar called from the side of the nearly completed shed. "Bring 'er here to me. I'm dying for something to drink."

Lucille shaded her eyes and called back. "Yes, yes, presents for you, Monsieur Edgar, and your helper too. Sunshine tea and bits of tongue between bread."

"Adrien? Adrien! Hey, Boy, come wet your whistle."

From the small loft area Adrien called down, "Coming boss." He pounded his hammer twice more to drive home the nail. Behind him, where sharp rays of sunlight made columns of dust motes, he heard a monotonous humming. He twisted around. "Who is that? Who is there?"

"No one. To hurt you," said the voice that was Lily. "Someone to. Help you. I, help others find, what they want."

"Okay, come on out, let me see you." Adrien's strong voice belied his uneasiness. His scalp was crawling because, try as he might, he couldn't make out the shape of the person speaking.

"I. Can help you."

"This is stupid! I won't stand here and listen to a — " He was cut off by the voice, so close to his ear it made all the hair on his neck stand up.

"You need, not shout. Nor stand, for that matter."

Suddenly Adrien was sitting on the unfinished floor. The faint sound of Monsieur Garance hammering down below grew still. He could hear Madame Lucille laughing at something her husband said. Adrien inhaled deeply. There was pine resin oozing from the fresh lumber. He squinted, then squeezed his eyes shut.

"When I open my eyes, I will see who is here," he said.

"Is, that what you want? You. Want to see?" said Lily.

Adrien turned his head without opening his eyes. "Yes, this is a dream, I can tell, I must be hungrier than I thought and I fell asleep. You look like . . . like . . . "

"Yes?"

"Anyone. You can be anyone, whoever I like. It is my dream. I can make you . . . "

"Yes? Someone. Anyone. Anything."

The silence thickened between them. Adrien wasn't entirely convinced that the shadow voice was a dream anymore. He was afraid, but the tickle in his throat signalled excitement as well. The prospect of curing his father's drinking and all the rest of it, no matter how, was too good to be true. And there was Alice.

"Go on," Lily said. "Ask."

"You, ah, can you?"

"Yes."

Lucille called up, "Adrien, time to eat. Better make it quick, your mom called. She needs you back home."

Her voice jerked Adrien from his reverie. The voice became smoky ribbons, evaporating as sibilant laughter into the columns of sunlight.

"Be, be right there, Madame," Adrien called down.

He pounded his hammer once more on the already driven nail, then slumped and closed his eyes. The voice was gone. The only thing left was the pine gum smell and the drone of bees outside somewhere. He stood and ran his hands lightly along the roughed-in wall. He turned from the wall and walked toward the hole in the floor that led to the ladder and down. His ears strained to catch that voice again. Nothing but the sound of an empty loft in an unfinished building in the heat of summer. He stared, as if hypnotized. The ladder was twelve rungs down to the main floor. Twelve steps, straight down.

If he fell from here, he would break his neck. He would die. The flies would find him first, then the dogs. Wait, if he was lucky the dogs would go find help and he would not die! Maybe he would end up a cripple for the rest of his life, and someone would feel responsible and take care of him, make it up to him, forever. This thought cheered him and he swung down the ladder, whistling.

Lily stirred in the corner. She watched the beautiful sixteen-year-old boy fall from view.

Funny, how they equate falling with, at best a fear, at worse a punishment. One is always falling into misery, into a depression, or on hard times. One might fall to one's knees; in prayer or in shame, fall in with a bad crowd, fall in love. And of course the greatest despair of all, falling from grace. Falling from grace . . . priests have used that one forever to control people.

Now and again, though, there are some who see falling for what it is, an opportunity. These chosen ones embrace the darkness. Not because it is bad, oh how tedious that train of thought, but because they relish the weightlessness, the freedom from fate. For one shining moment they finally have control over their own lives. How grand that step, to leap. To finally trust enough to fall.

The walls, beaded here and there with resin, began to shine. Attracted to the smell, a bee entered the loft and began her cursory investigation, antennae twitching, looking for the story. Lily whispered to her, sharing the boy's request and the promise made one summer's day. The bee tucked this into her back pouch and deposited a drop of honey as payment, as was the custom. She winged her way home, pushed by Lily's breath.

Lily had no substance with which to savour sweetness. Sweetness was the one thing she craved and the one thing she could no longer enjoy. She could no longer taste, only remember. That was the judgement levied against those who fell.

THE CAR HAD BARELY COME to a stop before Lucille flung open the door and stepped out. She steadied herself for a second then forced herself to climb the porch steps one at a time. She knocked at the door and Juliette was there, hugging her around the waist. She almost walked through Juliette and Alice both to get to her baby. She watched as Émérentienne finished the first round of prayers and tipped Bella's head to the other side. A small rivulet of blood came out of the nostril. She held back a sob. The girls kneeled, as she kneeled, beside the table, adding their voices to Madame's barely audible prayers.

Outside on the porch, Edgar held Maurice. Adrien was leaning on the car and watching as his father came towards them from the barn.

"Garance, what's all the noise for?"

"Bella has a nosebleed."

"All this for a nosebleed?"

"She can't stop sometimes, you know that. She might . . . "

"No one dies from a nosebleed, Garance. Not around here for sure. The old lady'll fix her up. She knows what to do. Am I right? You can pay me later."

"I can pay you? *Depuis quand?*"

"Depuis now, I figure."

"You son of a bitch."

Philip Trefflé crossed his arms across his chest. "Now, now, not in front of the kids, eh? Wouldn't want them to think we aren't friends. Listen, why don't we talk about this over, say, a glass of something? You are a man who pays his debts so besides the pig for the party, well now we have a little matter of this help. I reckon . . . "

"You reckon I will pay you for your wife's prayers? Is that what you are saying?"

"No, I am saying you'll pay me for your daughter's continued good health."

Lucille stepped onto the porch. "It is done. She's all right. She will be all right. Edgar, please, come help me get her to the car."

Edgar went into the house and left Trefflé in the bright glare of his son's stare. "We have work to do," Philip said, and punched Adrien on the shoulder by way of steering him towards the barn.

Once Bella was settled in the back seat, the other kids piled in and Edgar drove slowly out of the yard.

As he approached the barn, Adrien slouched down a bit and smoothed his face until it was still as stone. He blanked out the turmoil roiling inside him, in case his father would, as he often could, read his mind. He coughed, spat and mentally pitched his voice lower. Cap pulled down to hood his eyes, he circled away from his father towards the side door and entered cautiously.

He was struck by the warm, metallic tang of blood in the air. From a rope and pulley on the ceiling swung a large sow, her distinctive black spotted face almost obscured by the blood still dripping from the belly cavity. Under the body was the galvanized bucket burlapped in ice to hold and clot the blood. His mom made the best blood sausage in Autant, and his mouth watered at the thought of boudin on toasted bread. But, it was too hot now to butcher, the meat would spoil.

"Boy! Did the Devil give up before bringing you brains? Get over and get to work. Get this stuff packed with salt before the fuckin' flies and maggots make a mess in there."

Philip tipped back his chair in the shadow and gestured towards the carcass with a half empty bottle of leftover liquor made from soaking the insides of a whiskey barrel. When they were still in Gaspé, his dad had called it *l'eau bénite*, holy water.

"Me and Joseph have been busy already all morning," he continued. "Got the side room boarded up."

Joseph Corneille looked up at the boy and smiled. He was washing his hands in a bucket with yellow soap and a scrub brush. A jean jacket and empty coffee cup on the bale of hay beside him.

"What's that smell? You eat something?" Philip tapped the bottle into his son's chest.

"Sandwich over at Garance's."

"Well, there'll be *boudin* for supper I say. No need for handouts from them any more. You get over here and do a man's job. The other job a man's gotta do," he said, cupping his groin. "Einh, Corneille?"

Joseph half smiled at the gesture. "Sure, Boss, whatever you say." He poured himself a shot from the bottle. "This pig's going to Edgar's tonight?"

"What does Monsieur Garance need a pig for?" asked Adrien.

"Let's say, I traded him a pig for some lumber. I . . . " A low roll of thunder interrupted him.

"Better make this quick," Joseph said, draining his cup. "Storm's rising."

Adrien rolled down his sleeves and steadied the swaying carcass while his father took up the knife.

BELLA WAS FEELING A LITTLE lightheaded so she did not put up much of a fuss when Lucille insisted that she stay in, and in bed. She allowed her mother to plump pillows that smelled like Heet (her dad's) and pipe tobacco (her mom's). She smiled when her mom lifted the sheet high and let it parachute down over her, but her head started to hurt again and so she shivered and was still. Lucille gave her a glass of water with some Eno and a bowl with a bit of water on the bottom in case she had to throw up. She kissed her on the forehead and left, softly closing the door.

"Well, it is just the two of us now," said Ruel. "Welcome home."

Without opening her eyes, Bella sighed, "Who are you?"

She does not recognise me? Me, she does not know? Her reaction was so unexpected that he forgot to hold onto the hazel green colour he had chosen for eyes. Now his eyes had no colour. Now, they were black, shiny wet black. His short curly hair was the colour of the sky. His features were angular, his skin grey as bark.

Bella sat up, and looked at him. "Who. Are. You?" she asked again. She leaned over to squeeze his wrist a little like Alice squeezed hers when she was angry, but she wasn't angry, just curious. "Have you been here before?

Do I know you? Are you a dream? Why is your hair blue? What's the matter with your eyes?"

"What do they call you now?" asked Ruel. He knew the shape and true resonance of her light. No mischief could alter that.

Bella opened her mouth to answer, then shook her head, no. If ghosts or even others called you by your real name, it was very difficult to get them to leave you alone after that.

"No? They call you No? Strange name to give a child, yet it would solve the eternal problem of children doing what they should not, going where they should not go, eating what is forbidden."

"My name isn't No. My name is Bella . . . oh!" She clapped a hand over her mouth. *He tricked me.* "What's your name?" she said quickly. "It's fair. You know mine."

He hunched over, to accommodate her size. "Ruel — it means Small Road. We are one small light on one small road leading home."

Bella sipped at her Eno water. The headache rumbled in her stomach. "Lectric lights or candles? I like candles, the light is soft and more yellow and I can have one of my very own at the table if I am careful. The wax sometimes falls on my hand though when I carry the candle. It burns." Bella held up her right hand and pointed to a thickened patch of skin below the knuckles.

Ruel tsked and took the glass from her. "Not firelight," he said.

"Lectric then," Bella said, scooching closer, cross-legged beside him.

"Love. Light as love." His hands wove the figure eight on its side. He made Marie-circles in the air.

Bella watched Ruel's story curl and unfurl, sounding like bed sheets snapping on the clothesline, like sails on a tall ship. She saw then. He was from far away and he was here to take her, home. *That is silly. I am home. Oh, away home. What?*

Ruel's hands collected their story, their unfulfilled contract, up into the shape of a bee and carefully placed it in the bag tied to a belt around his waist. Bella heard a contented, busy humming sound coming from the pouch. Ruel smiled, his eyes relaxed into blue cat's eyes. Bella decided she liked those eyes best and she patted his hand.

ALICE HAD BEEN GIVEN A chicken of her very own. The eggs that chicken would lay in time, she could sell. It wouldn't be much, but a fortune for a thirteen-year-old girl. She named the chicken Roméo. A romantic name because it was part of the name of her ever-true love, Adrien Joseph Roméo Trefflé. She planned on a new dress, even went so far as to tell her mother, a dress of red plaid. The same material she saw him fingering in the store last time they were there.

Lucille snorted. "Red plaid? Lumberjacks wear red plaid, not little girls. Besides, it is the middle of summer and that material is too thick. Save up your egg money, ma belle. Later, if you still want to buy yourself some nice material, I'll teach you how to sew. It is a good skill to learn anyway and high time you learned. But plaid, Alice? Honestly."

Alice had already spoken to Madame Toupin and asked her to put aside the material. There was the promise of eggs all summer to keep Madame happy.

Now Juliette heard her mom promising Alice another chicken as reward for having been such a quick thinker, such a responsible sister, and she was livid.

"Mom, it was me who . . . " she began.

"You did your best, Juliette. You tried. Thank you, ma fille. Now, find Dad. He needs to butcher chickens for tomorrow. We can pluck them tonight and soak them in ice. One less thing to do tomorrow."

"Mom . . . "

Lucille poked at the clothes already soaking in cold water and absently began to unbutton her own shirt. "I need to check on Bella and get a quick supper going. Toupins are coming tomorrow instead."

"Um, Mom?" said Alice.

Lucille looked at her blankly. Alice gestured toward her hand working the last button.

"Oh. Yes." Lucille laughed, shrugged out of her shirt and dropped it in the pail. She pulled down on the front of her bra and adjusted a strap. "I need another shirt," she said, before quietly opening the door to her bedroom, where Bella was.

Alice shook her head and busied herself wiping the oilcloth on the table. "Juliette, did Maurice find my knife?"

Juliette fingered the knife in her pocket. The sharp point threatened to pierce her thumb. She slid her thumb over the blade to the smooth handle. The handle was a hard, dark glossy piece of polished wood. Smooth handle, easy to handle, to handle another way, to hand her the knife, hand her, handle her, use the knife.

"Well?" Alice straightened and looked directly at her sister.

"Alice, *viens-donc ici une minute*," Lucille called from the bedroom. Alice scowled at Juliette and went to her mom.

Bella drifted past her into the kitchen, holding the almost empty glass. She offered Juliette the last sip of

Eno. Juliette took the glass and swirled the milky pool at the bottom and drank it.

"Can I go play?" Bella asked.

"No," said Juliette. She looked at her sister through the bottom of the glass.

"Why not?"

"Because."

"Because why?"

"Mom wants you to stay quiet. No more blood. You scared her, Belle, with the creek and all that. *Compris?*" she said, bringing the glass to the sink.

Bella looked up past her sister. *I could tell Juliette that this one doesn't feel like ghosts. No sadness, no taste of salt. This is spicy like a pickle.*

"Bella, did you hear me?" Juliette said.

Bella said nothing. Ruel was putting his fingers over his mouth, the old be-quiet sign. She sighed and went back into her parents' bedroom.

Supper that night was perogies, garlic sausage and a salad from the garden. Léah and Joseph were there. The three children did their superhuman duty and did not fight or bicker or even speak unless spoken to. Everyone walked on eggshells and everything felt droopy. Bella was listless, withdrawn. When Joseph tried to make her laugh, she would have nothing to do with it. She slid her gaze across his face then down again with a sigh. Léah took her on her lap and rocked her, crooning and murmuring. Bella closed her eyes and allowed herself the luxury of near sleep, her stomach still roiling with saskatoon pie and Ruel's presence.

He chose to sit as far away from her as possible. From his place on top of the fridge he could see the entire family. Through grey wisps the family appeared as a constant to and fro of small lights, quite like stars and yet much warmer. Shades and grades of yellow, a small purple spot deep within Lucille, pink, orange, a green there, then the Bella pearl of calm white light.

It was intoxicating to be among them. "We get like this," Lily explained it to him, the last time they were here. He had been feeling quite off, unable to focus, or remember. She told him it wasn't so much the proximity as it was their peculiar vibration. "Quite different from ours, slightly addictive," she had said almost lovingly. It was true. There was something raw and rough about them, almost obscene really, how most of them could operate on sensual alone. Not a familiar element to be sure. How to accomplish a task when objects kept moving? When the lights twitched, dimmed and then sparked anew, as if of their own free will? Why all this grey they were surrounded with? The veil, a euphemism he had heard of, was as confounding as it was wearisome.

Mistakes could be made, accidents. Consequences could be disastrous. Wrong lights being dimmed, wrong lights sparked up again. Tiring, painstaking, finicky work but he was born to it. He only needed more practice. If he were to retrieve the Bellalight, he would need to keep focused on her and her alone, no matter how many distractions whizzed his way. No matter that even through the grey, there was something, something tantalising, a sweetness there in that yellow glow. He could almost . . . almost, what was the word? Taste. Yes, he could almost taste something as Lily said he would if he stayed here long enough. It was a frisson more than a quantity — it was a distraction. He needed to keep sharp. He pulled open his pouch and sent the bees out.

❧❧❧

GOD IS GETTING HIS HAIR cut. Truth be told, he could do it himself, it's a quick job, same length all over with the clippers, but he likes having his head massaged. He is dozing, half in and half out of the world when Coyote slips into the shop and sits down. God smells him.

"So, what news?"

"Well, seems our people are neck in neck."

"You mean neck and neck."

"No, neck in neck, or arm on arm, whatever."

"I don't understand."

"Well, it's like this . . . "

❧❧❧

"Son of a bitchin'." Joseph scooped a bee off Léah's shoulder and bumped open the screen door to throw it out. "Crazy little bastard figures you're a flower," he said, looking back at her.

"I am sweetness, dress on, or off," whispered Léah. She kissed Bella's forehead and stroked her back.

"That's truth," he said, feeling around his shirt pocket for a smoke. He patted his pants pockets for a match then grabbed the box from on top the coat rail. Edgar clapped him on the shoulder on the way out and together they sat on the porch to smoke.

77

Lucille got the dishes sorted and left Alice and Juliette and Maurice to it. She poured the dregs of the teapot into her mug. "Merci," she said, offering the mug to Léah, nodding down at Bella: "She seems quiet now. *Pauvre puce, einh?* It's tough on her."

Léah shook her head at the tea. "No, thanks. Tough on all of yous not knowing if she'll . . . "

"Yes, well, we are used to it by now." Lucille started for the bee circling her daughter's head then thought better of it. She settled back in her chair and sipped at the tea.

Léah cocked an eyebrow, pointing her chin towards the bee.

"Leave it," said Lucille, remembering how this afternoon she'd felt a little better, a little lighter, after the bee had travelled her arm. "Is Joseph all right now?"

"Yes, he said he was going to talk to Edgar about it. So I dropped it."

"Yes, of course. Play some cards?"

"Sure, let me put her down first."

Bella said, "I am awake you know. I'm not a baby."

Lucille laughed softly, "Sure, Bella, sure. Come on, come on, come on. Upsy daisy. Let's wash your face and get you to bed, big girl."

Lucille took her hand and together they passed under Ruel's gaze. Bella looked up and so startled Ruel that he spun off the fridge and almost landed on the floor. His wings brushed the mug off the table. Eyes snapped from blue to black.

Bella laughed for the first time since they'd brought her home from Trefflé's. She winked at Ruel.

Joseph and Edgar sat on the stoop. "You know you were right. It was that crazy alkeyholic stole the lumber," said Joseph.

"Yes. Thanks for that."

"Myself, I helped him put up an extra room on that shack of his."

"Huh, that was quick."

"It wasn't much really, just a nine-by-nine add-on. Pretty much roughed in, he still needs more lumber and tar paper and whatnot to get her right."

"So we watch out for more stuff disappearing."

"You know, Toupin'll figure it was me but what the hell. I want to spank out our shack too."

"Probably a good idea. The sooner we get that done, the sooner Toupin will be off your back."

They rested against opposite rail posts and drew up a list of things to buy and plan, two smokes worth by the time Juliette, Alice and Maurice came and plopped on the stairs at their feet.

Juliette pulled on Joseph's arm. "Watcha doing?"

"Building a castle."

"Can I see?" said Maurice.

"Sure. She ain't much but . . . " Joseph quickly added lines and a cigar shape to the list.

"Looks more like a cabin than a castle," said Maurice.

"Oh, does it? What about now?" Joseph drew a turret and a moat all around the place.

"Nice, very nice," said Maurice.

Joseph laughed and tucked the paper in his shirt pocket. "Come on, Monsieur Maurice, let's go see if your old paps here has anything worth stealing in that shed of his."

Edgar teased back, "Let's start with moving some lumber." They went off to the shed, Maurice howling like a coyote in the wheelbarrow.

Alice said she figured it was time to make sure the chickens were shut up for the night.

Juliette said, "Hey wait, I'll do it for you."

"What? Why? Like you would do me a favour."

"I feel bad about today, you losing your knife and all, okay?"

"You didn't find it, did you?"

"Well, mostly."

"What do you mean, mostly? How can you mostly find a knife?"

"I mean, I know where it is, okay? It's in the creek. There was no point going in there with the muck all stirred up and crazy like that. I'll go tomorrow and find it. Promise."

"Juliette! By tomorrow it'll be all rusted, it'll be ruined. God, you are such a pain."

"Fine, I'll go get the fucking knife right now if you need it so bad. As if you ever even use it. Go kiss your chicken beddie-bye, okay?"

"You little freak."

"Me freak? You freak. You love that chicken more than Adrien will ever love you."

"Juliette, I'll go get my knife from the creek myself. You kiss the chickens, I mean put the chickens in the coop."

"Whatever."

"Freak."

"You freak." Juliette turned and stomped away. She turned to watch Alice disappear into the windbreak, then danced a little jig that scared the chickens back into the coop.

Secretly, Alice was thrilled to be able to walk to the creek, knowing that Adrien sometimes went there to fish after supper.

She could hear him singing before she saw him, the song about the prince killing someone's favourite swan. She smoothed her hair and started whistling the same tune so he wouldn't be startled. Sure enough, a blank face had replaced the singing by the time she was beside him.

Alice asked if he had fished out a knife. When he looked at her closely, she felt the blood rise to her face and hurried through an explanation of the afternoon.

"So, you carry a knife with you, but not now. No knife," he said slowly, looking at the surface of the creek.

"Juliette said it was still out there, somewhere in the mud."

"I'll keep my eye open," he said and cast again, and handed her the rod. He reached into a canvas rucksack beside him and pulled out a mason jar. After a slow full drink, he wiped his mouth with the sleeve of his shirt and nodded toward her. Alice nodded, and he passed it over.

She wiped the rim and took a sniff. She wrinkled her nose and held the jar up to the slanting sun. Exactly the correct colour. Same as her mother's. She asked him where he had gotten it, knowing and hoping he had stolen it from his own father's stash. Her mother only made enough for family and family friends after all.

Adrien shrugged and reached for the jar, drinking half of it in one more go. He screwed the lid back on and, fumbling, put it away.

They made small talk about the weather and school starting up in September. They would be in different grades of course, but shared the same hallway. Adrien filled her in on the details of how the grade tens had stolen the five-foot Virgin Mary at the end of that hallway. She knew most of the story but hadn't realised the whole grade had been threatened with expulsion if they didn't bring her back in one piece.

"Old Tremblay was shitting bricks, I tell you!" said Adrien. "He said to bring her back, but he didn't say where, so we left her in his garage. And the garage was full of nudie pictures and not just calendars, right? He didn't tell anyone and neither did we."

"That's why you weren't expelled?" asked Alice, pretending she knew what nudie pictures were all about.

"Pretty much," he laughed. "Anyway, all we wanted was to kidnap Marie in return for a day off school. A little fun right? And well, now we know where to go to look at boobs and snatches."

"Oh right, snatches. Um, and what about Marie?" asked Alice.

"She made it back, all in one piece. So deal's a deal. Done is done."

Alice shivered. The sun was long to setting but the mosquitoes were already out humming and hunting. She slapped a few from her legs and arms and finally, when he seemed to be out of story and words, she stood up. "Well, I better get back."

"Yup, me too. See you soon, right?" He pulled himself up. His hand took hers and squeezed roughly.

"I suppose so," she said, smiling, and tried to pull her hand away.

"Say yes, Alice." He squeezed a little harder.

"Yes, sure," she said, feeling the blood race into her face. He let go of her hand. She put her throbbing fingers to her cheek and turned away. "See you," she said. She heard him grunt and unscrew the lid of the jar.

She knew if he found the knife he would give it back to her, surely, maybe. Probably he would give her whatever she asked for now.

Thursday

JULIETTE LET THE COOP DOOR slap shut. "Maurice? Where are you?" she called. She shook her head, searched the yard for her brother, a chicken under her arm.

"Here." Maurice's voice came from behind the scrub-brush pile between the house and the coop. He had wandered away from the men when they seemed more interested in the jars in the shed than the lumber. He didn't want to move jars because he was afraid he would drop one. He was clumsy they said.

"Mom wants two chickens for supper tomorrow. You and I get to butcher them, come on. I have one. Bring that one." She waved towards the chicken pecking Maurice's running shoe.

He stared at his sister, jaw open. "Mom wants us to kill Roméo?"

Juliette bumped his arm with her elbow as they walked towards the stump and the axe. "Yes, we need chickens and, plus, we need to put old Roméo out of her misery, you see. Alice loves this old chicken so she can't do it. Roméo is sick and won't live very long anyway."

She placed her chicken on the stump and, clucking to it, drew a line with her finger across the stump, mesmerizing the chicken to stillness. Maurice handed her the axe. As she stroked the chicken's back, she pushed its head down.

She placed her foot on the head while Maurice positioned himself to hold the legs. He pulled just enough to stretch out the chicken and give Juliette a clear shot at the neck. It was a tight fit with the two of them hovered over the stump, but the axe was sharp and Juliette was strong. She brushed the chicken head from the stump and Maurice tossed the body a little ways over. Roméo jumped towards the carcass, cackling and pecking.

"Sick? How is Roméo sick?" Maurice picked up the chicken and set her down on the stump. He began to trace a line in front of Roméo's beak.

"This chicken is suffering. You can see that. She is all tired, look. Look at her eyes. Her eyes are half closed all the time. See here, how crooked the nails on her feet are? Sure sign of a sick chicken. And this last thing, it isn't a pretty sight, but you need to see this to understand how sick Roméo is. She has big lumps under her wing. Feel." Juliette lifted the wing of the half-sleeping chicken and by stretching the wing up a ways, made the tendons stick out. "Letting a sick chicken back into the coop isn't good for the other chickens. All their feathers will come off and then they will have sunburn and die."

Maurice recoiled. "Oh non! Pauvre Roméo." He lifted a grubby finger and smoothed the top of the chicken's head, stroked her beak. Juliette was glad to hear the crack in his voice, to see tears welling in his brown eyes. "Pauvre, pauvre Roméo," Maurice said. A heavy tear plopped the dust in front of him. The chicken snapped out of her trance at the sudden movement. She fluffed her chest feathers and tried to pull back her wing. A large wing feather came off in Juliette's hand as the chicken squawked and tore herself away. "Oh!" Maurice's hand went to his mouth. "Oh! She is losing her feathers! That's not good!"

"Hurry up and catch her," said Juliette. "Come on, Maurice!"

Maurice took off after Roméo. Juliette's face lit up with this new mischief.

RUEL SAT ON THE WINDOWSILL; Bella was on her own bed upstairs, playing with her doll, Léah-banane.

"Because she has a nose like a banana, see? and ma tante gave her to me."

"Why Léah?" Ruel asked.

"Silly, she's my ma tante," Bella said. "She comes over to visit my mom and me. We talk and play cards sometimes. She sees the people I do sometimes. She plays pretend with me."

Bella paused and looked at Ruel. He was wearing a dress after all, and a purse thing. "Do you?" she asked.

"Do I what?"

"Play? Play pretend?" Bella asked.

"Yes, you would see it as that. Yes," said Ruel.

"Do you play house or church or school? Like us?"

He turned his face away from her. He seemed sad about playing pretend; the corners of his mouth turned down a little. She searched for the right words, something to make him feel a little better.

"Alice sometimes still plays, she gets all the good parts. She is the teacher when we play school, the mom in the family." Bella giggled. "Sometimes, she makes me be the dog."

"You can be whatever you want to be?" asked Ruel.

"Yes." She paused. "What would you like to play?"

"War," he said.

Bella had a flash of silver before her eyes, much like the bread knife blade glinting in the sun, but bigger, and it burned in her mouth. She quickly shook her head.

"Cowboys and Indians?" he bent a little closer to her, pretending to check the hem on his sleeve. He watched her die again, a blow to the head.

Her eyes widened and watered, the headache came roaring back. As she fumbled for the barf bowl, he straightened and sighed. She croaked and a small spool of spittle hung between the side of the bowl and her mouth.

This was going to be more difficult than he had planned. It would take more time. He propped his face in his hands, elbows on his knees. He smiled and pulled the pouch open. With one hand he rolled the contents around the bottom of the bag.

"Whatcha got there?" she asked.

He blinked back at her. He had the eyes of a frog. He blinked again, one eye brown and one eye green.

"Don't be scared," she said. "It sounds like little rocks. Marbles maybe?"

"Bees," he said.

"You have bees in your purse?" asked Bella. She smiled. "My mom sometimes has bees in her pocket. She says they go in there for peace and quiet. She said we talk too much. Do you think I talk too much?"

Ruel closed his eyes. *Her. Her light. The light, such light.* "Your mother has bees?"

"The bees belong to Dad. He built hives for them. Can I see yours?"

He tipped the open pouch towards her. Bella saw stones, small, lustrous honey-and-blood coloured. Eight glittering beads. She put her hand in and rolled them beneath her fingers, greeting each one in turn. Bella remembered a bee she had found one day helping her dad near the hives. At first she'd thought it was a stone because of its lustre and size, the golden colour closer to mead than your typical bee colour. She slipped off the bed and reached for her special-things box on the shelf, next to the plastic statue of la Vièrge Marie. Placing it on the bed between them, she lifted her eyes to Ruel and said softly, "My bee is like these yellow ones, maybe yours are her sisters?"

Ruel prised the lid from the Pot of Gold box and Bella pushed aside the white chicken feathers, the magpie feathers, and in the corner was the bee. One of the virgin sisters God had made.

He began talking to himself, quickly and hushed, as if praying, "God couldn't be here all the time and he was curious, in a fashion, about the state of earth, so he fashioned ten bees from the warm golden wax of his ear in order to hear the goings on of the world. He sent nine out to gather human memories, promises, works of awe, acts of love, sweet stories: 'Gather the goodness of these people and bring it all back to me.' This bee is from that first generation.

"The second generation became diluted. People spent less and less time loving and feeling simple awe. The land filled with smoke from forests on re and agriculture began. The bees were starved for sweet, for goodness, so they feverishly concocted their own, collecting pollen from flowers and making honey. And once they imbibed honey made from the earth, they became more kindred to earth than to spirit. They were intimate with geography and places and so nested everywhere, mated with all manner of creatures and stayed. The original sisters still report back to God on the sweet places and thoughts. God is aware of the changing earth, her trees, flowers, wind, water, beasts and, of course, her humans."

Ruel delicately motioned towards the cover of the box. "The next family of bees is like this Madame here. She holds a box with a picture on it, and the Madame in the picture holds a box with the same picture and so on. The real box is here and the others are reflections of the real one."

"Like an echo?" asked Bella. Struggling to concentrate on the Lady on the box because if she thinks of the bee, surely Ruel would insist she give it back. After all, it belongs to a family and families stick together.

"Yes, but imagine an echo with a sweet smell and a warm taste."

"You know," Bella said, "our bees make honey in the hives. They like it here." She holds her poupée closer, pressing it against her roiling stomach.

"Do you know how bees make honey?" Ruel asked.

"No one knows that. It is too dark to see inside the hive, and the bees are too small."

"Not at all, not at all. One has only to be the right size, then . . . "

" . . . pretend?"

"Pretend," he said. He scooped the bees from the pouch and, with his fist, slowly wove a figure eight. "One young bee gets the flower water, the nectar from a worker from outside. She finds a quiet part of the hive. Here she sits, as you do now, opening and closing her mouth as you do, exposing the juice to the air. Water evaporates from the juice. The juice thickens into . . . " He finished, pointing his fist at Bella.

"Honey!" Bella clapped her hands in delight and tapped his fist.

"Yes." Ruel laughed and opened his hand. "Honey."

Bella drew closer, stretching a tentative finger over the bees. She felt them shiver. They were alive and warm. "Oh, they are beautiful. Do you think my bee would like to 'bee' with her sisters? Or will they fight? My sisters fight all the time. But they would be lonely not together . . . " she trailed off.

Yes, please, yes. It has to be offered.

Ruel cocked his head towards her, their heads nearly touching, before a whisper of something that sounded like tinkling glass chimes breathed, and the bees in the pouch simply rose between them and flew off, out of the open window.

"Why did you send them away?"

Ruel sighed. "I did not. They are sometimes called, sometimes merely capricious . . . their job is to find stories, and so . . . " He lifted his hand to encourage the bee in the chocolate box. He waved towards the window, but the bee remained still.

Bella carefully replaced the lid and said, "I know where they might go. Come on, I'll show you." She propped her doll back up against the pillow, got up off the bed and reached for Ruel's hand.

Ruel stood and brushed the back of his hand against hers. He smiled at the fizzing sound between them and then slowly, luxuriously, stretched. His wings fanned out. They were magnificent, bright as a full moon and rising slightly higher than his head.

91

Downstairs, Edgar welcomed the Toupins and started pouring drinks for the men. They groused about the dismal crops. They complained about the dry spell they were having. All that thunder and no rain, it wasn't natural. A neighbour's cows were sick, drinking from the same slough they had drunk from for years. Two wells had gone dry and even Léo Charrois, the diviner, could not find water. The people were confused. They felt betrayed and angry, like they had fallen from grace.

L'abbé Breault and the town council had decided to organize a party, la Fête au Village, to help shake off the bad things. A pit was dug for a pig roast; corn was to be trucked in from Falher and trestle tables put together. A baseball game would be organised in the school field for the young men. The older guys would have a horseshoe competition in the churchyard, with the priest's blessing, of course. First prize would be a new blue fuzzy car blanket. It had a picture of Marilyn Monroe on it.

Trouble was, some of the older women wanted to play as well, there was talk of a round robin, but a girls-only tournament was voted in. Lucille had donated beeswax candles and a sly jar of honey mead under Léah's table-cloth and four napkins. An offering. The gift basket was packed and ready in the cool house.

"Oh ma chère, I love how you roast a chicken, for me it isn't too spicy at all. To go through the trouble of having a hot oven on today and what with yesterday . . . Well, that makes you *une véritable sainte*! Who is the patron saint of cooks? Sainte Anne? It must be. She's the one to pray to on behalf of the house, at any rate. We should say a prayer of thanks to Sainte Anne and then the blessing for this meal we are about to eat."

"Ah Florence, I was taught that Sainte Marthe was the saint for cooks and, besides, I am partial to Marie for any intercession. Don't be too kind in your praise of my wife's cooking. Too much richness can't be good for the digestion, einh?" said Edgar. He looked up from the chickens splayed on the cutting board before him and gave his wife a wink.

Lucille was grateful. Her husband's easy way with people, his ability to turn even Florence Toupin's snide remark into a compliment, was a gift. She touched him briefly between the shoulders when she came up beside him with the bowl of potatoes.

"Where is our Bella?" asked Edgar, taking the bowl and sitting down. "She isn't one to miss a meal."

"She still isn't feeling well. Her headache is nearly gone but she still seems out of her plate. I gave her some honey on toast and milk with molasses. She is upstairs."

Edgar picked up the carving knife and cut into the second chicken. "We had quite a little adventure around here yesterday, Toupin. Bella found out that she couldn't swim like a fish." Edgar winked at Alice. "And our Alice here found that she could. Lucky for us one of them can!"

Alice beamed. Juliette stretched her leg to kick her, but her mother's hand was on her shoulder. "Yes, Alice is so responsible. She is growing up, that one." She squeezed Juliette's shoulder a little harder and walked on. Juliette scowled.

"Our little Bella," Edgar continued, "is the roamer in the family. We need to tie her down or put rocks in her pockets. We might lose her yet, some day, einh? But not today I think." He looked at his wife. He knew he was missing something, felt it in her clipped tones and the sour look blooming in Juliette, but he decided to leave the females to their battles.

"You are the lucky one. I can't get any of mine to ever leave the house," said Hector Toupin. He poured gravy over his entire plate of food.

"Dad," said Séraphin, "I asked you today if I could go fishing and you said no. Said I had to work because Corneille wasn't there to unload the mail."

"That's Monsieur Corneille to you, Boy. And, you need to learn about the hard work of running a store if you're to take over some day."

"What about me, Papa?" asked ten-year-old Estelle. "Will I take over the store?"

"You? Non, *Chérie*. You won't be stuck in this godforsaken place," said Florence. "You will be a teacher. There will be no village store for you." She busied herself cutting Estelle's meat.

"Now, it isn't all that bad, is it?" said Lucille. "You own the store out right, don't you? Run the post office and the lumber mill. Hector is the village constable. And Florence, you have raised fine, decent children."

Juliette wondered if her mother's words were pointed at her. She snuck a look, but Lucille continued, without looking at her. "Estelle could do worse than to marry one of the boys from here and settle down. She could teach here too. Someday, people from all over Alberta will come to get their honey from us. Someday, Autant will be the place everyone talks about."

"I am grateful for your generous retelling of my business, Lucille. However . . . " began Florence.

Hector recognized his wife's familiar tune gearing up to explain what was so wrong with Autant. "Listen to her would you, Edgar? 'Autant will be the place people talk about.' Like as if we have a gold mine here," he said, spearing a potato.

"Well now, Hec, that is something I need to talk to you about. We just might have a gold mine here. More honey-coloured than golden, but still. After supper we'll take a walk to the west pasture. Show you the new hives. The size of the colony has doubled since last month. A new batch of bees must have hatched. The clover, dandelion, and willow around here did amazing things in the spring and now the fields and gardens are doing the job. We need to talk about shipping some of the honey out. I don't think we can sell it all in the store."

"Do you really think it's worth putting money in honey?" Hector worked his fork between plate and mouth regular as a clock ticking. "It's all very good on toast and pancakes, but this wine you make . . . now that is something special."

"Honey won't give you gas like sugar can, and it has uses you never even dreamed of. Now that this batch is doing so well," said Edgar, "I was hoping you would be able to help me bottle and sell it as medicine."

"Medicine? Are you crazy? What can a little sticky stuff do that good old cod liver oil or some liniment can't?"

"Lucille and I have been doing some experimenting and you can use honey for all kinds of things. Did you know that it can be used to cure meat? They do that in Germany.

They use honey to dress a wound there too. Lucille rubbed a bit on chilblains and it healed them right up.

And," he paused dramatically, "a tablespoon of honey will take care of a migraine. You know those blistering bitch headaches you sometimes get? Well, think if honey could be used for such a headache!"

Hector grunted. "Be easier to swallow that than the *tisanes* the old lady forces down my throat at any rate, and pills just make me sleep."

"Exactly!" Edgar was excited now that he had found a receptive audience. "Straight honey on a boil — which is just pus, like water, anyway — shrinks that ugly blot to nothing in about two days. No messing with raw potatoes or castor oil. Lovely sweet honey alone will do that for you."

"Can we please not talk about this at the supper table?" said Florence. "Just thinking about bees makes me shiver. Dirty bugs. And those stingers! I don't know how you can stand them!"

"You have to be sweet, not like you, you old dried up old *cue de poule*!" Juliette whispered to Maurice, tickling him. He twisted in his chair, keeping his head down.

"What was that, Juliette?" her mother asked. "Keep your elbows off the table. Maurice, you haven't even touched your supper. Eat up or no dessert."

Maurice lifted his shiny brown eyes towards Alice. "Alice, I wish I could be like you. You are so brave."

"What?" asked Alice.

"You. You are so brave. Already a second helping. Poor Roméo." His eyes filled with tears and his lower lip trembled.

"Mom, can I go check on Bella?" asked Juliette, lifting her voice over Maurice's.

"What in the world is the matter, Maurice? Great big boy like you, blubbering like a baby. Who is Roméo?" asked Florence.

"Your family goes to pieces at the slightest provocation. Must be all the women in this house," said Hector. "Not like my boy, einh? Steady as a rock!" He thumped Séraphin playfully on the back.

Séraphin was following the unwritten law of the table, whoever eats the fastest gets the most. His father's hearty clap made him choke.

"Are you trying to kill your own son?" Florence leaned back in her chair and slapped Séraphin hard between the shoulders.

"Raise your hand to open your air pipe," said Estelle to Séraphin holding up her own to show him how.

"Juliette, what is Maurice talking about? Why is he crying about Roméo?" asked Lucille.

"Dad?" asked Juliette, head below the range of her mother's piercing look. "Dad, *s'il-vous-plaît*?" she whispered.

"Juliette said Roméo was sick, we had to kill him," blubbered Maurice.

Alice's face paled and she dropped her fork on the table. She stared at the chicken heaped there, snuggled under her mom's good brown gravy. She put a hand over her mouth, shooting daggers at her sister.

"Are you going to be sick?" asked Estelle. "Here, use this." She held out her napkin.

Alice buried her face in her hands.

Edgar Garance looked at Juliette. "Who should we take care of first?"

Juliette hung her head. Somehow things were suddenly complicated. Edgar rose from the chair and motioned with his chin for her to follow him.

She followed her father to the porch, head down. She would pay for killing Roméo. *Better sooner than later and better Dad than Mom. Sister Régina was right when she said that God watched everything. Is he watching out for Bella and Alice too? Or is it only me who gets his eyeful today?* She sniffed miserably.

Edgar sat on the porch step, pulled out his small pipe and the flap of tobacco. He took his time preparing the bowl, tapping down the tobacco, and then handed Juliette the match, wordlessly asking her to light it. She scratched the match along the rock on the top step, put there for this very reason. Sulphur flared and she breathed in the yellow plume, exhaling it like he'd taught her. She smiled up at him, hopeful.

He didn't smile back. She handed him the match. He snapped his wrist to extinguish the flame. "Your arm," he said.

Juliette pulled up her sleeve and bared the delicate underside of her arm. Her father touched the still hot match to the skin of the wrist. Juliette clamped her mouth shut and didn't cry out. It was like a bee sting, a sharp, small hot pinch, throbbing like something alive had been jabbed under her skin.

"It won't leave a mark, but you will remember it was there. That is what sin is, fille. It leaves no mark, but you know it is there. Between you and your sister, there is a mark now. It won't go away by itself. You need some help to make this right. Now, what will you do?"

"I don't know," whispered Juliette.

"Think," said her father.

"I could ask for help," she said through clenched teeth.

"Yes, yes, you could. What would you ask?"

"For Mom to take away the pain," she said.

"She would need to know why you were burned and then what you would you say?"

"I would tell her and she would laugh, because she hates Alice anyway?"

Edgar sighed. "Juliette . . . "

"She loves Alice, I know. She loves her and she hates me. Mom would say it isn't right to hurt people."

"You are right, it isn't right to hurt people. But you are wrong to think Mom hates you. She knows you will eventually do the right thing. Which is?" asked Edgar.

"Put honey on it so it doesn't scar."

He lit another match and lit his pipe.

"Honey would do the trick. And that's what you need, a little sweetness in your thoughts, your actions, in how you treat your sister. Brother and sisters. Compris?"

"Yes."

From inside the house they heard Florence spitting about disgrace and shameful behaviour and how it was Juliette who had caused Séraphin to choke in the first place.

"You have made enough supper conversation I think," Edgar said. "Go to your room and be with Bella for awhile. After supper is done for everyone else, you can come with us to get some honey." He tapped the pipe against the step.

He winked and this freed Juliette. Her father did not hold a grudge. It was done with him.

She scooted off the porch steps. She climbed the stairs up to their room and saw Bella wiggling her way out the window. "Shit-sakes, Retard, what are you doing?" She gently pulled her sister back in.

Although there was slim chance the little one could have gotten through, Juliette knew she would be held responsible if Bella fell. "Bella! What are you doing?" she said.

Bella looked wide-eyed, but she was asleep. "We are going to visit the bees," she said.

"Who we? What are you talking about? Belle, you are dreaming." Juliette knew better than to shake her sister when she was like this.

Bella yawned and picked up the leather bag Ruel hadn't had time to retrieve before Juliette walked in. "No, I am not dreaming. I have friends, you know." She looked at Ruel who sat quietly on the stool on Alice's side of the bed.

"Like hell you do. Hey, where did you get this old thing? Is it Alice's?" She took the pouch from Bella and stretched it open, sniffing the inside. "What was in here?"

Bella shrugged. "Bees," she said.

"Beads? Ashes and burned things more like it. Cigarettes butts. Bella? Are you smoking?" Juliette tucked the pouch under her mattress.

"Hey, that's mine," said Bella.

Juliette slapped her hand away. "Finders keepers. Anyway, you stole it and stealers can't be choosers. Move over."

Ruel's eyes were blue again. Bella shook her head. "Not now. Later," she whispered.

"Shut up, Bella." Juliette yawned and plucked a book from the low-slung shelf before flopping onto her stomach to read. Ruel looked longingly at the pouch, its ties dangling free, and reached for Bella's doll instead.

Downstairs, Alice's sobs were reduced to hiccups. Lucille gave her a mouthful of honey wine in the bottom of a teacup, much to Florence's dismay.

"I would certainly never give my children alcohol," she said. She was organizing the table; plates stacked one on top of the other, spoons together, forks all facing north.

"Oh, Florence, a drop won't hurt her. It was a shock to hear about — " she looked over at Alice's tear-stained face and sighed " — it was a shock. This is just to calm her down. She won't get drunk. Flor, stop messing with those."

Lucille reached over and gently touched the other woman's arm. "Come, sit awhile. Let's pray for a miracle and maybe the damned dishes will do themselves for once."

Florence opened her mouth, but something in Lucille's face stopped her. Her mouth snapped shut as she peered closer. There were dry, dark circles under Lucille's eyes, a strained look at the corners of her mouth, the telltale swelling round the breasts.

"So, when is it coming?" she said, sitting down.

Lucille smiled thinly, sat down facing her and poured a teacup full of wine for both of them. Now that the men and children were gone, there was a shift in the rapport between the two women. They were no longer upholding family virtues or protecting husbands' reputations. Now they were simply two women, neighbours, almost friends.

Alice recognized this and reacted by sliding a little lower down on her chair. *If they forget I am here, they'll keep talking. I have never heard them talk like this before. I thought they hated each other. What do grown-up ladies talk about? What does Madame Toupin mean, "When is it coming?" What is coming?* She studied the bottom of her cup.

"Ah, not for a while," said Lucille. "*Février* early, I think. Maybe fin janvier."

"A winter birth. Winter isn't the easiest time to get to the hospital," said Florence, taking a tentative sip from her cup.

"Not the hardest either," said Lucille. "I think I can remember what to do. At least I will have the time to do this one properly. Bella was born la fin d'août, just in time for canning season. What a mess that was!" She put the cup down on the table and smiled at Alice. "Do you remember that, Alice?"

Alice looked up. Like a deer caught between the lantern and the knife, her eyes darted from her mother's smiling face to Madame Toupin's surprisingly softened expression. Today, all the ugliness must have meant something. It was good that Bella didn't drown, of course. Roméo's death must have paid that off. She could only nod. Her mother smiled back and patted her hand across the table.

Florence chuckled. "I, for one, certainly remember that day. When I arrived I thought there had been a murder! Edgar's mother on the floor, you spread out on the table here and what I took to be blood splattered from one end of you to the other. Who would have thought the old lady would faint from the heat of the stove? She had never fainted a day in her life, that one. Touch of the influenza, as I recall." Florence sipped again.

"Yes, it nearly killed us all that year," said Lucille, swirling the contents of her cup. "And I never did put up that last batch of beets," she laughed.

"Ah yes, to bloody beets," said Madame Toupin. She raised her teacup and the women clinked cups together.

"What a mess," said Lucille. She poured another measure into Florence's cup.

"And how do you make this?" asked Florence, eyeing the liquid in her cup.

A ray of west sun slanted through the window and trapped itself inside the bottle on the table.

"There was a recipe, that came with the first batch of bees." Lucille walked over to the shelf by the door and retrieved Edgar's bee log. She flipped to the front part and found the slip of paper glued there for safekeeping. She smoothed out the cahier in front of Florence.

"Huh," said Florence. She quickly scanned the recipe. "This," she tapped her tea cup, "is not that. Not by a long shot. Would be a different colour for starters if you don't boil it."

Lucille laughed. "Well, I had to skip a few parts and added some tartness. Too sweet otherwise."

"Someday you must give me the actual recipe," Florence said. Her tight smile cracked open to swallow another mouthful of the amber-coloured wine. "For now, it would be nice to think there was a bottle or two of this for la Fête. With l'abbé's blessing, of course."

"Of course there will be. And of course, his majesty requested and blessed it. Along with a few jars d'eau forte."

103

"Amen to that!" Florence touched her cup to Lucille's and they smiled.

Lucille stood and began to scrape the bowls into the garbage pail. "Alice, time to start the dishes."

Alice, numbed by the conversation that had passed deep and quick as churning water between the two women, blinked and struggled out of her chair towards her mother.

"Oh thank you," she said, hugging her mother's waist.

Lucille was taken by surprise by the sudden burst of affection. She had no idea why her daughters behaved as they did, reacted as they did these days. *Give me another boy.* She kissed the top of Alice's head. *Boys are so simple.*

Alice hesitated in front of Florence Toupin, ready to hug her as well. But Florence's all too familiar pinched expression had returned, so Alice grabbed her hand and shook it firmly.

Madame Toupin's jaw dropped and she puffed herself up to ridicule the girl. Lucille put a finger to her lips, not wanting to embarrass her daughter.

↝↝↝

COYOTE AND GOD ARE PLAYING double solitaire. Coyote studies the four cards, flips over the queen of diamonds, and slaps her on the King. He signals the bartender for two beers.

God waves him away. "No, thank you, I'd rather a nice tea."

"Are you sure about this?"

God looks him in the eye. "Yes, I find a nice cup of tea to be quite . . . What are you after?"

"Nothing, nothing at all, it's just . . . Ruel? You send a puppy out there, for this? I'm not messing around this time. Lily is on the job for me back there you know."

"It will be fine, he needs the experience. I see great things..."

"Me too. I see great things happening for me!" Coyote barks and laughs. He stands and slaps two coins on the table. "One pays for the beer, and the other is a tip for you."

"A tip? For me?"

"A yup. Don't fuck with me. I lost her once and I will not lose her again. I mean it."

"Keep your money, Coyote. You will need it to buy more beers, to drown your sorrows." God flips the last card and, although it is against the rules, lays the jack of hearts over the queen of diamonds. He feels the queen bee shiver inside his sleeve.

Friday

THE NEXT MORNING, EDGAR WAS up early to check on the hives. He stopped at the shed for his smoker. It felt to him as though all his bones were melting, his insides turning to soup. He found a shady spot on the other side of the shed and rolled himself a cigarette, amazed there was enough spit left in him to seal the paper shut, and squinted through the trees. Early morning really and already so damned hot.

Females are peculiar. Juliette so mischievous and getting downright mean. Lucille jumpy as a tic. When they synch their bleeding, I will have to enlarge the shop and live there.

He settled himself more comfortably on the ground, stretching his legs. He inhaled and blew out smoke rings.

If Lucille would get pregnant again, everything would settle down. She'd quit worrying about Bella so much. Ah, we make good babies and Bella's almost six now. It isn't for lack of trying. We try all the time, always on Sundays if the weather's bad and the kids are asleep. Maman was dead wrong about her. She is not evil. Hasn't killed me in my sleep, grabbed all the money and gone off drinking. She is a strong, smart-as-a-whip woman, and maybe, yes, a little too set in her bush ways for some people's liking. All that talk about spirits and Coyote and such. Well fuck them and anyone who looks like them. When that woman walked into my life, everything got better.

It wasn't the best beginning . . . so drunk that I just wanted to sleep after that party we had when Toupin's fencing was done. Lucille, dark angel, came to me under the wagon. Pulled off her dress and just lay there. Said I was calling her, that I was a stone she would pick up and put in her mouth to tame. Stone or not, I was rock hard. And she put me in her mouth all right. I will never forget that part.

He heard thunder. He blinked up at a clear blue sky. *Storm still a ways off.*

He pinched the cherry off the end of his cigarette, squished the ember completely under his boot and pocketed the stubby for later. *I pray for rain but if there is going to be a storm, I better get to the hives and back double-quick.* He began to whistle and walked a little straighter down the road. His sex hardened at the thought of maybe another party when his own shed was done and, perhaps, another go at the stone in the mouth.

He dreamed on about honey, the hives and the queen. Approaching the windbreak, he saw from the corner of his eye the shifting grass shadow of a coyote moving behind the hives. The coyote sat on his haunches between bars of shadow and light.

He noticed something else, approaching from the west, perpendicular with the windbreak, though with the sun at that angle, it was difficult to see clearly. He shaded his eyes. *A person, a very tall person with long, wild hair. The hair spread out behind, like wings. A giant of a woman with wings. Imagine that! She's waving. Whatever it is, it can't be a woman or that tall. Wings? Wait, there are two heads now, and who's that laughing?*

107

The sun sifted light through a blanket of cloud. A shadow darkened and disappeared and two small girls, his daughters, not more than three hundred yards away, were coming through the field, parting the wheat, to reach the hives ahead of him.

The girls, of course that was it, trailing a blanket. A trick of the sun, them so tall with a blanket billowing out behind that looked like wings.

"Hi Dad!" shouted Bella. "We came to see the bees!" She ran towards him.

His face broke into a smile. "Allo, la Belle! Come here, come to me."

Juliette hung back. She and the coyote regarded each other, her dark blue eyes resting on his honey yellow ones. The sun rose a little higher, brushing them all with a coat of pink-red-gold cloud. Summer was buttoned with roses and dripping with bleach along the edges. The coyote howled. The air filled with a sudden wall of smell and the sound of bees.

Edgar was hunkering down to receive Bella. He twisted up when the smell hit him. The peculiar odour wending itself from the hives was panic and fear. *Sapristie 'pi tout les saints . . . there's only one queen.* "She's going to swarm!" He stood and ran towards Bella who had just crossed in front of the hives. He lunged to save her from the brunt of the impending rage.

Thousands of bees broke to the surface. The hives boiled over with gold, black and brown bodies. The colony rose in a roar, lifted as one mind, one voice, but what purpose? Edgar threw Bella to the ground and rolled over her. They lay face down in the grass. The bees dipped low over their bodies, hovered for a moment then honed in on Juliette, standing still just behind the hives.

The coyote delicately stepped away from the windbreak, sniffed the air, then loped towards the bees. There was a crack of thunder. He leaped and was swallowed within the swarm, became part of the swarm.

Juliette would forget about the coyote and remember how she'd caught Bella's eye as she peeked out from under their father's arm before the bees flew over them and descended upon her like rain.

From where she watched, it looked to Bella as though Juliette was wrapped in a luxurious chenille blanket.

Instead of being warm, Juliette was cool. Thousands upon thousands of small wings were fanning her. She shivered and a ripple went through the colony. Every hair on her arms, every nerve in her body received the sound. It blotted out everything else. She wasn't afraid. She forgot to be afraid and listened instead to the sound. Her mouth was shut tight and covered with bees navigating her face. Her ears were muffled and filled with the song bees sing in their hives to welcome and encourage their new queen. Her eyes were shut and the patterning of a million small feet gave her a map to wonderful places. The musky scent of hives and honey, community, unyielding and forever, told by wings and clawed feet, every colour reflected through all the facets of one eye.

The bees shrank, tightened their grip on the girl. They stopped moving. Stopped fanning as another layer of bees settled on her already sealed body. She felt heat; fire was filling her up completely. She stopped breathing. One voice was clear through all the bees.

this o n e she goes allto flame clean brighthot freeh er
from thehive clean thedistancebee tween one and the next

The bees lifted from her. She fell to the ground, lungs bursting for air and saw through glazed eyes the swarm, dark as deep water, sway up and through the trees, taking with it all the colour and sound from the world. She lifted her head up off the ground and spoke in a voice she did not recognise, "This is not over. We are not afraid."

She righted herself. Blundered her way towards her father and little sister who were already struggling to stand and reach her. She saw the angel with blue hair. She heard him say, "This is not over. We are not afraid. We are walking in light, we are walking with the light. This is not over and we are not afraid."

MADAME TREFFLÉ AND ALICE APPLIED cold tea bags to the stings and Madame and Lucille recited promissory prayers to St Bernard de Clairvaux. To keep Juliette from cursing, Lucille decided that some honey wine might be a good thing and liberally poured her two cups, one after another.

Juliette lay on her bed, eyes closed against the spinning in her head. Bella's singsong voice talking softly to her friend, the angel she saw at the hives. She could hear adult voices downstairs rising and falling, "The child needs to rest and drink water." Her father's rumbling voice each time the screen door opened, saying hello to Monsieur Toupin, her mon oncle Joseph, ma tante Léah, Monsieur Trefflé and Adrien. She slowly drifted towards sleep with Bella curled up beside her. She rolled to her side facing the open window and listened to the conversations both inside and outside the house.

Ruel, silent now, sat on the stool, wings tucked against his body, precise as a Japanese fan. Pouch tied to his waist again, his blue eyes were ticking between the girls on the bed by the window. He held Léah-banane and absently stroked her hair.

As the adults poured coffee and rehashed the day, Alice looked over at Adrien. He winked and they slipped out the door, onto the porch.

"Alice, you're pretty smart for a girl," said Adrien.

"What do you mean for a . . . "

"I mean you are smart. To save Bella the other day, and now Juliette all full of bee stings."

"Bella — you know that when she bleeds we need your . . . "

Adrien continued in a rush as though he hadn't heard her. "Wanna watch the fireworks? Tomorrow? With me, I mean? We'll sit on the hill by the school. I did that last year."

Alice looked at him, her nose wrinkled in consternation. "I'll ask my mom, later. Tomorrow Juliette and I have to pick the raspberries. Or maybe not. Maybe just me. Mom and Dad want to be in town early. How about I meet you in the old barn before? I can tell you for sure then."

"Okay," he said. "What do you say though? You want to come?"

"Sure, if I can," she said.

The door swung open and Philip, Joseph, and Edgar stepped out. The children pulled themselves back into the shadow between the door and the window.

Philip lit a cigarette and Joseph used his fingers to blow snot from his nose over the porch rail.

Edgar said, "Joseph, unless you want to suffer the wrath of the women in this house I wouldn't blow mucous all over the flowers."

"You are whipped by the women in this house," Joseph said.

"You want to tell Lucille that?" asked Edgar.

Joseph didn't answer. Instead he said, "Let's get that pig out of the truck. Where do you want it anyways? I got other things to do tonight."

"Corneille, it's my pig and it's dead. What's your hurry? We got all night and hauling pigs around is thirsty work," said Philip.

"I believe it belongs to the village now," said Edgar, "and it needs to be delivered to the pit because the coals have been going since this afternoon. That pig will need a good full day to cook. We want to eat before the fireworks." He didn't wait for an answer, just turned around and walked back into the kitchen to tell Lucille they were leaving.

"What do you mean you have something else to do? What else is there? You work for me, Corneille," said Philip.

"I work for who pays me. Yesterday, Toupin. This afternoon, you. Don't matter to me," said Joseph. "Give me a smoke there."

"Get your own smoke, Big Man," said Philip. "You got so many jobs, got people paying you, I should be bumming off you."

"Don't be a stingy asshole."

"Okay, let's go," said Edgar, stepping back onto the porch, hefting the wine they had started earlier.

Hector Toupin was behind him, trying to put his hat on straight. "I'm coming too," he said. We should stop at the store, Florence needs . . . "

"We're not stopping at the store. Fuck Florence," said Philip, flipping his butt into the darkness. "I'll drive. There isn't enough room for all of us, stay here, Joseph Corneille. Or better yet, get lost."

He pushed his way past Joseph and down the stairs.

"Might not be a bad idea, with moving things and all," Edgar said. He touched Joseph briefly on the forearm and gave him the wine. "Don't drink it all in one go. You have river work to do tonight." He winked.

"Edgar, that boat'll float whether I am drinking or not," said Joseph. He clomped down the porch and headed toward the windbreak.

"Good guy. For a Métis," said Hector.

"He is a good man," said Edgar. "Are you steady there, Hec?"

"Steady as a, whoops! missed a step there, how many steps you got around here anyways?"

Edgar laughed and nudged Hector down the steps and into the waiting truck. Alice and Adrien breathed a sigh of relief.

"Well," Adrien said, "at least I know where my dad will be tonight. Let my mom know. Don't forget, tomorrow, the barn." He took the four steps at one go and landed in the dirt without a sound. He turned and grinned back at Alice, then sprinted out of the yard.

Upstairs, Juliette rolled over, closed her eyes and started humming. Ruel's eyes snapped from blue to black and he tightened his grip on the doll.

Saturday

THEY MET IN THE BARN, that sixteen-year old boy and that thirteen-year old girl. Adrien had spread a horsehair blanket over a broken-up hay bale and they sat together, side by side.

"I hear Joe Nault gave a second pig. Pretty good feed tonight I think," said Adrien.

"Yes, there's always a lot of good food," she said. Correcting him quietly would save him the embarrassment.

She fiddled with her hair and told him she had braided it the way he liked, just for him. He reached out and stroked the long braid, colour of clover honey. So blond it was almost white. Then he gave it a tug. Clicking his tongue he called her his little pony and Alice laughed.

"A little pony in the barn . . . that's a good one! I have to go soon, Mom and Dad are already in town. Dad had some things to do with the parade, and mass is in a couple hours. I promised to do the dishes for Mom so she could talk to L'abbé before mass."

"What does she need the priest for?"

"To get Bella blessed again this year."

"How is she?"

"Mom said it's a drip that won't stop. She keeps swallowing it. Can you imagine? Being so scared of something that you keep bleeding? Dad got stung on the back of his neck. Juliette is hardly swollen at all anymore."

115

"Yes, I can imagine some people being scared like that. I can imagine blood. Juliette is lucky. Bella, she's . . . "

They were quiet for a moment. Outside, the birds kept singing, and flies buzzed around the doorway. A bee flew in through shafts of light. Lighted on Adrien's arm. He didn't flinch. Just held the arm up to Alice.

"Figure this was the guy who bit your dad?" he said.

"No. They die after they sting someone, you know."

"Yah, well, this one is dead too," he said. Chuckling, he trapped it, pressing hard. His laughter died as he raised his hand from his arm. *She wants it.* He suddenly found he was hard. The bee reared and flew towards Alice. She shrieked and he slapped his hand over her mouth. "Don't scream, they'll hear you," he breathed.

He grabbed her by the braid with his other hand and forced her down onto the blanket. He covered her mouth with his. Pawed across her chest, kneading her tiny breasts. Pulling and pommelling. He fumbled at her waist, pulling up her dress. Searching.

Alice wrenched from side to side. She bucked and slapped at his arms. Punched his back, but he rolled on top of her and the weight numbed her, pinned her into a silence.

His pants down, he braced himself, his arm over her throat. "You are mine so act like it. You like it." He pushed against her, tearing the panties.

Hardness entered her. Jagged pump followed jagged pump. She turned her face from him. Numb. There was tearing and there was the little wet blood. Finally he groaned and pulled out.

She wasn't trembling anymore. She said nothing, head still turned from his. He rolled off and got to his knees, pulling up his pants. *Done is done. What you wanted. What she wanted.* He looked at her; he felt as dazed as she looked. He pulled her braid softly. "Alice? I . . . are you okay? Just shut up about it, right?"

She curled up, away from him, pulling her dress down as best she could. She said nothing.

He touched her shoulder and she winced. He said, "That's just what people do. You know that, right? Alice?"

"That's not what people do," she whispered. "That's animal."

He stood and fastened his belt. "You asked for it. You know that, don't you? You know that. Come on, get up. Don't be a baby. It's fine. I love you now, right? Okay? You are mine and no one else can have you. That's it, it's done. Alice?"

He kneeled back down and stroked her hair and helped her up. The panties were around her ankles. He gently peeled them away from her feet and put them in his pocket. "Mine now, right?" He grinned.

She nodded.

He smoothed the shoulders of her dress. "Now, you get yourself to la Fête. Wait a minute. Fix yourself first." He pulled straw from her hair. "I'll see you tonight, and no one needs to know about this, right?" He chucked her under the chin. "Alice, look at me."

She looked at him sideways. Her mouth trembled. She crossed her arms over her chest and nodded.

He pulled a cigarette bent and broken from his pocket. "Let's smoke to seal the deal. That's what they do." He lit the cigarette and shakily took a puff. He passed it to her and she shook her head. "Come on, it's fine. It is good, we're okay. Come on." He held the cigarette to her mouth.

117

She leaned forward and took a small puff. She coughed and choked.

He took a drag. "Yah, it is harsh the first time," he laughed, "but you get used to it. Here, have another."

She took the cigarette and brought it to her lips. "It hurts," she said.

"Not forever," he said, "not forever. Just the first time." He barely looked at the cigarette before dropping it to the ground. He fussed with her hair some more and checked her mouth closely. There were red marks there and where he had held her across her throat, but they would fade. He took her hand and led her out of the barn.

The wounded bee circled the smouldering cigarette. She flew around until the flames licked straw, piece by piece, up to the horsehair blanket.

The soft crackling from the barn floor was joined by an equally determined rustling noise from the hayloft. Juliette emerged from under the remnants of an old tarp and blinked, swaying in the light. She bent in half and placed her hands on her knees, trying to slow her breathing and her racing heart. She had stayed back, hidden, away from the edge of the hayloft. She had wanted to catch Alice doing something really bad for once. So, for once, precious Alice would be in trouble, but once they started, started that . . . what would she tell her mom they were doing? She didn't have much time. She would have to hurry to catch Alice before she got to town, to la Fête. Stepping toward the ladder, she stopped. Smoke, she could smell smoke. They had been smoking down there.

Now for sure Mom would kill her. Perfect! She swung around, her foot searching for the first rung.

A bee landed on her cheek. Instinctively, she swatted at it with both hands. She lost her grip on the ladder. Her hands scrabbled for purchase. Her foot missed the rung. Her feet scissored the air and she hung there motionless for a heartbeat, and fell. She landed on the back of her head. Her delicate neck cracked.

The bee moved towards her.

Ohnow mouse shit hay dirt clean brighthot freeh er from thehive clean thedistancebee tween one and the next

Maurice banged open the door to the shed, panting and heaving. A shape uncurled itself in the corner. "Juliette? Is that you?" He lurched forward and threw himself onto the shadow.

"*Tabernacle*, get off a me!" said Joseph. "Have you gone mental? Get off!" He rolled away from the boy's clutching embrace. "I am not your sister."

Maurice whispered, "Where is Juliette? She said she would be here until the bells rang."

"I came for some peace and quiet. To sleep." Joseph swiped at his nose with the sleeve of his shirt. "Maurice, what in hell?" He took hold of Maurice's belt loop with one hand and his arm with the other.

"Alice, she wants to kill me for killing Roméo. Don't tell her you saw me." Maurice shook himself free and raced out the door.

"Who the hell is Roméo? Not that fuckin' chicken?" Joseph said.

He rose to his feet, kicked at his nest, searching for the jar of wine. It rolled out from under his feet, empty. He sighed and stretched his arms up over his head. *Great. Looks like I slept half through the day. Just great. Kid'll tell Garance he saw me, I know it. Edgar'll know I didn't deliver the stuff. He'll tell Lucille about me sleeping in here, Lucille'll tell Léah and then Léah will kill me. Hostied pique!* He turned this way and that, stretching against the door jam, getting the kinks out of his back. The sky was a blazing clear blue, not a cloud to mar it and just a whiff of wind. *They say it is this clear sort of blue right down to Texas. Wherever that is.* A bee droned close. He swatted at it. A dog barked. He cocked his head, nostrils flaring. Smoke.

Leaning away from the shed, he looked up and down the farmyard. *Is Lucille burning garbage? No, that's not garbage. Maybe Edgar is burning bush? No, not today, not with* la Fête *in town. Everyone's getting to the church and ready for the party.* He swung himself out of the shed. *Where's it coming from then?*

When he saw the thin smoke curling from the barn, Joseph thought it looked a lot like a dog up on his hind legs, big as a bush coyote even. It was long and lean and seemed to be sniffing the wind. Then it was smoke again, lying flat on the wall like a bad cat. There was a whoosh of wind and the barn logs barked. He wondered about calling out, or running to get help. It was an old barn and worthless anyway, but the hay in there, they could always use that. Plus, with everything so dry these days, no sense risking the fire spreading.

He turned towards the house. He had to find Edgar, ask him what they should do. He was still a little drunk. Then he heard Maurice screaming. He turned and raced for the barn.

Maurice had run into the barn and seen Juliette on the ground. Her neck at an impossible angle. Bees swarmed above her. Like liquid in a jar, they sloshed to and fro trying to mend the rift around her. There was a tear made by some mischief. More and more bees arrived until the air twanged in a high stressed thrum. They fixed

121

themselves together and it looked like they were trying to keep the flames from Juliette. But their wings fanned the flames instead. Accidents happened. Mom said that when mistakes were made they would have consequences.

Maurice would always remember that sudden heat, and when Joseph pulled him from under a burning beam, it was raining flakes of ash.

Ash so delicate silver-white, it looked to Joseph as if the boy was covered with moth wings.

RUEL

BELLA LAY ON HER BACK on a patchwork quilt under the big spruce, reading a comic book. Her mother and father, not fifty feet from her, were talking with the priest about blessing our girl. That one kept shaking his head and her father had his arms crossed over his chest. Thunder in his face.

I sat in that dusty spruce tree and soon as she climbed up to share my branch I saw the sickly yellow spire of smoke.

"Hello, *Monsieur* Ruel du Ciel."

"*Bonjour*, Bella."

"Are you here for la Fête?"

"Non, ma petite, I am just here."

"Soon the bells will ring. The party could be for you, they could know you are here," she said. "It might be better if you weren't bees though." She looked down towards her mother. "After yesterday they are afraid of bees today."

"Only you are supposed to see me."

"Please, if we showed them, just for today? Mom, and maybe Juliette again? I think she forgot already. They're all sad and grouchy. If we showed them that you are here, they would be happy again. Do you see?"

"They would not be happy."

123

"Monsieur, even Dad prayed to God last night. If you would . . . Here, I brought you something." She stretched her leg to get at the prize in her pocket.

"Bella? What is it?"

She opened her hand and offered the last bee. "Hold her for me. You won't let me fall. I trust you. Watch."

And in that blink, I won. I held the bee and learned that when the soul is given freely, there is no pushing, no pulling apart or scattering.

Adults turned their heads, thunder slowly faded. Their bodies tensed as if bidden by coiled springs, by the turn of some key. L'abbé Breault held the mother by the arm as she stretched towards my falling Bellalight, a scream tearing her throat.

She was there, kneeling. Her lips made the prayer. Her hands formed the Marie circles. Bella threw up. She looked up at me and said the deep humming of my voice shook her stomach. She quickly filled with loosed blood then stepped delicately from the body. People saw a large brown and yellow chenille bag drift down from the tree. Everyone saw bees, Edgar's bees. They saw the swarm hover over Bella, then rise.

Such a column of thick smoke over that place now. I bent my head and wept.

I CANNOT LEAVE, THERE IS one mistake left to make. Here they are, my family of lights. This family, a peculiar constellation that has shifted too quickly. No, of course not. They move in accordance to the divine plan. Just so. Although, I have to admit, two missing from their circle makes an interesting difference.

That Lucillelight has purple inside her. He is a stranger. There is no need to bother him. Alicelight needs to be consoled. A rip in her pink, there. Not exactly of my making, but I did nothing to discourage it. Not paying attention when I should have been. I knew Lily was . . . enough. I was sent for another reason. *Ainsi soit-il.*

I feel the pull to be gone. I know I am going to miss this place. This stone orchard is littered with the bodies of white moths. I had no idea that our tears would manifest as reams of white moths. These tiny flickers of light, ratty and torn, now lie dead and dying on the ground and villagers take ginger steps through fields of them to weep near my family. The family, I mean.

The priest leads them through prayer. Words I can understand. Words starved for love. "I confess to almighty God, and to you, my brothers and sisters, that I have sinned through my own fault, in my thoughts and in my words, in what I have done and in what I have failed to do; and I ask blessed Mary, ever virgin, all the angels and saints, and you, my brothers and sisters, to pray for me to the Lord our God." Indeed.

Alice, look here.

Alice raises her eyes from the mounds of dirt that hold her sisters. She looks blankly at me, the stranger wearing rhinestone sunglasses. A woman in ridiculously high heels. Shiny red high-heels and a cigarette dangling from her black-gloved hand. I choose to play pretend, for Bella.

There is something I need to give you.

I click open my patent-leather purse and hand Alice a folded handkerchief. She takes the plump cloth and holds it at arm's length as though it smells bad. As if she can smell anything beyond the memory-stench of moths and lingering smoke from a burned-out building.

"Those are for you. For you, Alice." I fold my hand over hers. She nods but not really hearing or understanding. I tuck the gift into her little straw clutch. Impressing upon her the greatness I am bestowing, I feel my own vanity rearing pointy little horns. "When you get home, put them in a safe place. For later. There won't be any left in a little while and these ones are to start things up again."

"What are they?"

What sang you here will bring you back.

— letters from Autant

AUTANT, 2012

"LET'S UNLOAD THE TOOLS, BOYS." André hustles his sons. "Okay, where is the rototiller? What? I most certainly did say to bring the rototiller, and an empty half-barrel and three shovels. And now we need some gas or kerosene to burn it all. What all did you bring? Two shovels? For Pete's sake, les boys. Since when are two measly shovels considered enough tools? Pierre, go to the summerhouse and see if you can wrestle up at least one more shovel. Bring the wheelbarrow while you are at it. Roll ma tante's barrel clean and bring it closer to the house. Léo and I will scoot on home and get the rototiller and gas. We'll bring the truck. Whose idea was it to come in the car? I don't care if it is more comfortable, this isn't some holiday camp, you know."

Inside the house, André's voice fades to nothing. Urbain has already dug out the suitcase. Alice folds a towel on the plaster-strewn floor and kneels beside it, rubbing her hands slowly all over the leather and around the sides.

"Who did this belong to?" asks Urbain, hunkering down beside her.

"It belongs to me, it was my ma tante Léah's. She gave it to me a long, long time ago, when I was a child. Just because it hit Maurice on the head doesn't mean it belongs to him. He is here because I asked him to come and fix the roof. My roof. And it is my attic that the moths decided to fly into and die, am I right?" She fixes her nephew with a stern look.

"Yeah, sure, ma tante, sure. Do you remember how this opens?" He leans forward to pull the case upright, but Alice puts a hand on his forearm.

"Maybe underneath?" Urbain offers.

Alice isn't looking at him, or at the suitcase, not really. She is focused on something, somewhere inside the suitcase.

"Do you want to take it outside first? Is that what you want? Shall I lift it for you? Do you want me to take it outside and show Dad?" Urbain fumbles around with what he believes is the front. "There doesn't seem to be a handle."

"No," says Alice. "No, Urbain, sit down. You are my godchild. I want you to see this. I remember now. Of course I know what this is."

She places her hands on the sides of the case and the hidden latches spring open. A smoky perfume wafts out. She pulls open the tired elastic pouch from the lid of the suitcase. There is ma tante Léah's mirror and the beautiful pine lock Adrien gave her, shiny from use and only a little warped. The key is there as well. Alice feels along the silk lining on the bottom. Her father's bee log of course, and from the side pocket she pulls the handkerchief. She unfolds the yellowed lace and scoops up a handful of dark ruby and amber coloured beads. The beads stir in the crux of her palm.

Urbain's eyes grow wide and he leans forward. His aunt rolls the beads and drops them from one hand to the other.

129

Alice hears the sound of a match head being dragged against rough paper and the bees begin to glow and grow warm. The long breath of summer wind comes in through the backdoor left open. The wind walks through the house and gently wakes those bees. Alice lifts her hand up in the air and nine bees take flight. They have left a dusting of flower-coloured pollen on her hands.

Urbain hears the car crunch along the gravel in the driveway and wishes he were with them. Maybe his dad will let him drive home if he does this job properly. He saw a trick of light, his aunt threw a bunch of kidney-coloured beads into the air and they disappeared. He looks up, then checks the floor around him. In his stomach, the illicit mead sings a hello song to the pollen on his aunt's fingers; they are after all of the same family.

Maurice lets himself in with the wind, the door closing softly behind him. He hears Alice talking to Urbain in the living room. It isn't so much that he wants to interrupt them as he needs to hear the story again, for himself, to blow his brain clean of the images stuttering and stumbling like nightmares that smell too much like burning hair.

He eases himself onto a kitchen chair and props his bad ankle up on the garbage can beside the stove. From here, he can see out the window and into the yard, in case André comes back before Alice is done.

Alice is fluttering her hands as she tells Urbain about that summer in 1952. As she speaks she draws Marie circles, a figure eight on its side, over and over again. The circles gain pale colour in the telling, pink turning orange turning yellow turning green turning blue until finally a warm yellow light envelopes the two people. Every moth in the living room stained a different colour. Maurice blinks.

"Oh," Urbain breathes. "Oh."

"Yes," says Alice. She looks over at him, still slowly moving her hands through the air. "I had forgotten they were in here, how could I have forgotten? A lady angel gave them to me after the bees swarmed the summer Bella and Juliette died. Later on, I married your mon oncle Adrien, my husband before Roland. Adrien built this house for me. I must have remembered then, because here they are, in my old suitcase, in the attic, under the eaves. And I painted the front door blue. Do you know why?"

Urbain looks at his godmother. There in front of him is an old woman, playing with trick beads and flinging coloured powder about. As long as she is talking, he doesn't have to shovel moth bodies or move furniture.

He says, "No, why a blue door?"

"My mom always painted the kitchen door blue, so that angels would recognise the house as a safe place. I do it for her and my sisters. In case they ever decide to come back. They will recognize the door as a friendly sign and not haunt us. Not too much anyway."

Alice closes her eyes a minute and rests her hands on her lap. *I remember the colour of the angel's hair, the same colour as the sky. That's why I couldn't see her right away on the roof. She blended in with the sky.*

When she looks up, Urbain has lifted the bound papers from the suitcase and is rummaging through the silk pockets of the case. She gives a little grunt. "If you're looking for more, there are no more. Probably nothing in there but a penny for luck and maybe half a piece of gum.

Your mon oncle Roland loved his spearmint gum. That book was your Pépère's."

Before Urbain can say anything, there is a cough from the door. Maurice pokes his head through. He limps over to Alice, carrying a large glass of water.

"Here you go, la vieille. After that much talking you're bound to be thirsty."

"Merci, Maurice," says Alice, taking the glass. "Did you bring one for Urbain as well?"

"He's young. If he's thirsty, he can go get a glass for himself."

"That's okay, ma tante, I know where the glasses are," says Urbain. "Got to see a man about a horse anyways." He punches Maurice lightly on the arm as he heads down the hallway to the bathroom.

"Careful in there," calls Maurice, "the ceiling's liable to came down on your pecker."

"Maurice!"

"Well, it could," says Maurice, pointing up to where the ceiling used to be in the living room.

"Not that. Watch your language, I mean. You sound uneducated when you speak like that. Like a bushman or something."

"I am a man from the bush, Alice. And there's not too much smarts in this old head. Just had the brains knocked clear out of me, remember?"

"Yes, well, regardless. Urbain's young and very susceptible to influence."

"Whatever you say, whatever you say. Okay, so are you done here or what? We should figure out a way to get this place cleaned up." He stretches his arms out in front of him and whistles through his teeth. "Jaysus, what a mess. I hate moths even more now."

"Maurice?" asks Alice. "Are you all right?"

"Peachy. My leg's f . . . feeling better all the time." Maurice casts a glance towards the hallway. They both listen to the water running.

"Why do we never speak of it? It's not a very lovely story, that summer. But it ended well enough," says Alice.

"We got over it, but we never agree on what happened because I can't remember so much and you can't say too much because you weren't there," Maurice says slowly.

"Oh, yes. And the bees?" she asks.

"Yeah," says Urbain from the doorway, "What happened to the family bees, the honey monopoly in Autant?"

"Your mémère and ma tante Léah burned the hives, bees and all. Mom said it wasn't safe to keep bees anymore with children around."

"But near everyone around here had hives when I was a little kid," says Urbain. "Before they started dying off."

"Not us," says Maurice flatly.

"No, not us, but in Talon and Falher they all did," says Urbain. "Hey, ma tante, where are those beads you just had? The trick bees? Can I see them a second? I want to show mon oncle Maurice."

Alice blinks at her godson. Trick bees? Maurice catches her eye before she can open her mouth. He answers for her, "They must have flown away." He gestures to the roof, "through there, I suppose. Good for one trick is all they are."

Urbain follows his uncle's gaze and laughs. "Yeah I suppose so. Pretty neat-o trick, though. I wish the others could have seen that. They'll never believe me when I tell them."

"No," says Alice, "they won't."

"Come on," says Maurice helping, Alice to her feet. "Let's get out of Chateau Death. These moths are giving me the creeps."

"Chateau Death?" Alice picks up the cahier scrawled with her dad's handwriting, rolls it up and thumps Maurice on the thigh, and then she allows herself to be taken outside. "Maurice, honestly, you can be so dramatic." She fingers the small knife in her pocket.

Outside, Urbain relaxes in one wing chair after settling Alice in the other. Maurice takes up the bottle and picks off the plastic Five Star emblem before pouring honey wine into three cups. "Here's to your last bottle of wine, Alice. The boy is in for a peck of work when the others get back," he says. "It's only fair that he have a little refreshment now, einh?"

"Non," says Alice. She takes the mug from Urbain, defying Maurice to go against her wishes. "My house, my rules. He had some with his coffee already. My godson is no drinker. Are you, Urbain?"

The fourteen-year-old puffs himself up. "Well no, not too much. Dad sometimes lets us have a glass of wine or a sip of beer with supper."

"Every supper?" asks Alice.

"No, of course not. Just sometimes."

"You know that, Alice," interrupts Maurice, "you are at those suppers. We all are."

Alice softens. She leans over, touches his scarred hand. "I would feel bad for a long time if I led a child to drink. My first husband, Adrien . . . "

"Oh, for the love of God!" says Maurice. "You sound like Florence Toupin. Mrs. Holier-than-thou, Mrs. Never-touch-a-drop. The one who, it turns out, raised a pack of lushes. Nothing but drinkers in that family. Especially the girl — what was that little one's name?"

"Estelle," says Alice, smoothing her dress over her knees. "She married Guillaume Morisette, from Talon."

"And what about the older boy, Séraphin? Married that Pique what's-her-name. She left him after they lost the store, right? Burned it down for the insurance money, if I recall."

"Hmm, yes, now wait a minute, it was . . . Josée Pique!" Alice is proud of her ability to pull thoughts and names from thin air today. "Beautiful Josée Pique, she had the loveliest hair, always in a long braid over her shoulder, the colour of a crow wing. We are all quite different now, of course. We are memory-handsome."

"Hey hoo, you there!" calls André. He steps from the cab of the truck, waving. The boys begin unloading garbage barrels and a rototiller.

Urbain quickly drains his uncle's mug and sets it down near Alice's chair. He smiles at Maurice, who winks back.

"Get a move on there. Your dad needs all the help he can get."

Urbain wipes his mouth with the back of his hand and touches Alice's hand. "Coming, ma tante?"

"Yes, yes, I'm right behind you. Go on now, go."

Alice wrinkles her nose.

"Maurice?"

"Hmmm?"

"Did you smell that?"

"Smell what?"

"Urbain smells like wine," she says.

"He smells like all fourteen-year-old boys smell, Bella, like skunky creek water. And he smells like us, like good stuff that keeps us together, einh? Strong and sweet as honey."

Brother and sister help each other rise from the chairs. Arm in arm, they cross the lawn. A warm, smoke-scented wind hisses over the furniture, the glasses, and the bottle. It flutters the pages of the *cahier* left there.

BEE LOGS II & III
EDGAR JOSEPH GARANCE
1950 – 1952

janvier (1950) windy, cold, dark
Ordered more bees: 2 lbs. Asking about the queen — can she manage 2 colonies/hives? Can a colony survive without a queen?

mai — warm, windy cloudy near end of month
Total: 4 hives, how many bees? Who can tell?

août — hot and dry
30 lbs. of honey this time round. Lucille made honey wine. Pretty good. Even neighbours want some. This isn't Edmonton, there is no hotel here so buying alcohol is a solitary business. We aren't selling it high price as whiskey, maybe $4 a quart or so. That Liquor Board they set up is making millions for the government. Doubt a few hundred bucks here and there will be missed.

Bella wants bees, for a pet she said. Likes the sound she said. Handles them like a handful of raisins sometimes, pats them on the back for Pete's sake!

Lucille's other recipe for wine
1 gallon of water, 3 lbs. of honey, 1 lb. rhubarb.

Boil combined ingredients slowly for 30 minutes. Strain into earthenware crock, leave room for expansion. After mixture cools, add a tsp. of yeast for each gallon of water. Store in a cool place for 1 month. Cover crock with towel.

mai (1952) — warm, no wind
Total: 6 hives, there could be 10 to 30,000 bees per hive. I am not counting them one by one mind you, they make a ruckus. Already there are capped queen cells. New hives ready for when they split.

juillet — hot, some wind, dry as a bone
100 lbs. of honey. Moths a nuisance but bees keep them under control.

Lucille tried honey on Bella when she had a bleeding nose that wouldn't quit. She thinks probably the sweetness keeps the girl from going into shock. It's not right for someone to bleed like that, it's just not.

août — hot, dry, no rain, little or no wind most days
Bees swarmed.

Lucille and Léah burned the hives, unborn queens and all.

Bees have not returned.

⊱⊱⊱

GOD AND RUEL ARE SITTING at their usual table in the bar. It is late, later than either is used to. They are heavy into their conversation, heads nearly touching, shoulders hunched. Coyote shuffles over holding three tankards of beer. They slosh a bit when he sets them down. God looks up, absently dabs at the puddle with his sleeve. He looks back at Ruel and says, "Forgiveness is never a solitary act. You need to invite that person back into the room. It wasn't pretty the first time and is less pretty the second time. But necessity drives the car more often than pretty in my books, and it's time to motor."

Coyote laughs a sharp bark.

Ruel looks at him. "What are you laughing at?"

Coyote jerks his head towards the door. "Look who just walked in."

Ruel cranes his neck to see past Coyote to the door. God leans back a little and slips Coyote a folded ten-dollar bill. Coyote palms the bill and winks.

TRANSLATIONS

Ah bien — oh well

Ainsi soit-il — so be it

Autant — as far as, as much; also the name of this village

(ma) (la) belle — my pretty/dear one

bête — beast

bonhomme — (old) man

boudin — spicy sausage made primarily from pork blood

C'est assez — that is enough

(ma) chère — my precious one

(une) chouette — a baby owl, term of endearment

compris — understand, as in "Do you understand?"

cue de poule — the butt of a chicken

décembre — December

Dépêche-toi — hurry up

depuis quand — since when

l'eau bénite — "holy water", home-brewed alcohol

l'eau forte — hard liquor

(les) enfants — children

Enfant de la Terre — Child of Earth

Enfant de Christ du tabernacle — Christ Child in the tabernacle

(la) Fête — literally "the celebration" a village tradition in July to bless and keep the people and the village safe; begins with a mass, breakfast, parade, and so on (les) fille(s) — the girl(s)

Hostied pique — "host and pyx", pyx is the object used to carry the consecrated host or Eucharist, derived from the Latin, pyxis meaning box

janvier — January

Je vous salue Marie — Hail Mary, full of grace

Mademoiselle — Miss

(ma) tante or Ma Tante — my aunt, or Aunty

maudite bête d'enfer désespéré — goddamned beast from a most desperate hell

Mémère — grandmother

merci — thank you

Miel d'Autant — honey from Autant

(mon) oncle or Mon oncle — (my) uncle, or Uncle

Monsieur du Ciel — Sky Sir

non — no

Non, ma petite — No, my little one

pauvre — poor

Pépère — grandfather

Proche comme ca einh? C'est un beau marriage. — Close like that eh? Makes a good marriage.

(une) puce — term of endearment, literal meaning — lice

ragotte — alcohol made from soaking the insides of whiskey barrels

ramencheur — a healer, a fixer of broken bones (faith healer)

Sapristie 'pi tout les saints — literally "Saints preserve us" (la) senteur humaine — human semen

swish barrels — refers to the alcohol made from soaking the insides of whiskey barrels

Tabernacle — tabernacle, box in Catholic Church to hold the holy Eucharist

tisanes — herbal tea used for medicinal purposes

(ma) (la) vieille — my/the old woman

viens — come

viens donc ici une minute — come here for a minute

(les) vièrges — virgins

(mon) vieux — old man

Sources & Acknowledgements

Alberta Department of Agriculture, pamphlet, "Bee Keeping", 1973.

Detweiler, Tim, *Making Working Wooden Locks, Linden Publishing Inc., The Wood Worker's Library, Fresno, CA, 2000.*

Facklam, Margery, *Bees Dance and Whales Sing*, Sierra Club Books for Children, San Francisco, 1992.

Gojmerac, W.J., *Bees, Bee keeping and Honey*, Tutor Press, Toronto, Ontario, 1978 pp42-43

O'Toole, Christopher & Raw Anthony, *Bees of the World*, Blandford Cassell plc., Wellington House, 125 Strand, London, 1999

Pavord, A.V., *Bees and Bee keeping*, Cassell and Comp. Ltd., Cassell and Collier MacMillan Publishers Ltd., London 1975

Perlman, Dorothy, *The magic of honey*, Nash Publishing, Los Angeles, 1971

von Frisch, Karl, *Bees their vision, chemical senses and language*, Great Seal Books, Cornell University Press, 1963

Dr. Declan Unsworth, for his patience and thoroughness with medical concerns. Thomas Trofimuk for reading an early draft and letting me go off the deep end. Gail Anderson-Dargatz and Donal McLaughlin, for their invaluable help on earlier drafts and never letting me go too far off the deep end. Michael Kenyon for his editorial deftness and for bringing me back home.

Dedicated to mon oncle Arthur André Bussière (June 6, 1941 – August 22, 2014), without whom bigger mistakes would have been made.

For Raymond and André, the best people I know.

What if
the bees leaving
means angels are?
The lucky ones don't believe in angels.

Author photo by Raymond Blanchette-Dubé

PAULETTE DUBÉ's first novel, *Talon*, made the shortlists for the 1999 Canadian Literary Awards, the Alberta Writers' Guild Best Novel Award (2003), and the Starburst Award (2003). Her poetry has garnered a number of awards.